AIRborn

J. L. Ormord

Kingdom Books

Published by Kingdom Books, an imprint of *CreativeJuicesBooks, Singapore (www.creativejuicesbooks.com)*

National Library Board, Singapore Cataloguing-in-Publication Data

Names: Ormord, J. L., 1973-
Title: Airborn / J. L. Ormord.
Description: Singapore : Kingdom Books, [2015]
Identifiers: OCN 925578567 | ISBN 978-981-09-7313-1 (paperback)
Subjects: LCSH: Forgiveness--Fiction. | Families--Fiction. | Genetic engineering--Fiction. | God (Christianity)--Fiction. | Good and evil--Fiction. | Kansas--Fiction.
Classification: LCC PS3615 | DDC 813.6--dc23

Contents

For Nanny
For inspiring three generations
of storytellers

And for Ryan
May you forever entertain angels

Humans and Their Guardians

Roni Chambers — Priscilla

Jeni Chambers — Samuel

Juli Chambers — Ariel

Zoei Chambers — Priel

Ryan Miller — Oriel

Jason Miller — Oriel

China Miller — Neil

Allyson Miller — Anastasia

Trinity — Anastasia

Jared — Camiel

Jillian — Raven

Seth — Lorrel

Solomon — Saffron

James — Clayton

John — Daniel

Sarah — Rachel

Last Day at the Lake House

Six Years Earlier

"Forty-five, forty-six, forty-seven, forty-eight, forty-nine, fifty! Ready or not, here I come!"

The sun was setting as Roni began searching for her two friends, Jason and Ryan Miller. The last boat was pulling in for the night, and campfires began to come to life on the shores around Greenfield Lake.

Jeni and Juli Chambers, Roni's younger twin sisters, had just come out of the water after finishing a long day in the lake. They sat on the tire swing near the lake house, licking cherry popsicles that were dripping down their elbows and into the sand. Roni, Jason and Ryan had turned twelve last March and were given more freedom at the lake than they had ever had before, freedom that they decided to use playing hide-and-seek in the dark.

"You can't hide from me, Ryan Miller. I know where you like to hide," Roni shouted out.

She ran as fast as she could toward the cave which she knew was her friend's favorite hiding place. She waited patiently for him to make a move. She could hear Jason coughing in the distance. He was easy to find. She never went after Jason first, like Ryan did. She wanted a challenge.

Her legs grew tired from crouching for so long, so she stood up. When she did, a twig snapped, letting the whole forest—and Ryan—know where she was. He wasn't about to move now that he knew where she was.

Pretending to give up, she walked away. Then, with as little noise as possible, she began sneaking around to the other side of the cave, hoping to catch her opponent by surprise. Jason was still coughing loudly. Roni thought it sounded like pneumonia again. Quiet as a mouse, she crept up on her prey. She could see a shadow of him near the cave entrance.

"What an idiot," thought Roni. "As if I would fall for that trick."

She started inching forward. The cave was only ten feet away. She hid in the brush near the opening. It seemed like she had been waiting a hundred years, but Ryan didn't move. Finally she got up and walked over to where the source of the shadow was. Her anger boiled over when she discovered it was only Ryan's hat, stuffed with leaves and tied to an oddly shaped log.

"Ryan Allen Miller!" she shouted and kicked the log over, injuring her toe as she did. "You big cheater!"

As she hobbled back to where she could hear Jason coughing, she mumbled to herself, "That stupid jerk! He made me sit there forever, thinking I had him. I bet he was watching me the whole time!"

She heard snickering to her right. She stopped. The rustling of leaves made her whip around.

"I'm gonna get you, Ryan!"

She took off after him, forgetting all about her sore toe. Ryan could have easily outrun her but he held back just to tease her.

"Come on! You got me, Rapunzel!" he taunted her. He sped up to where she could no longer hear him crashing through the forest floor.

Roni stopped. She couldn't hear him anymore. She was exhausted. Leaning against an old pine tree, she tried to catch her breath. Suddenly Ryan jumped out from behind the tree and scared her half to death.

"Ryan!" she yelled and started swinging her hands at him wildly.

He held her at arm's length while she yelled and screamed at him. Eventually he let her go, and she ran head on right into his chest. He bear-hugged her and wouldn't let her go no matter how she struggled. He was laughing the whole time.

She finally gave up, leaned her head back, and closed her eyes. Her body went limp. Ryan, sensing an opportunity had come that would most likely never occur again, leaned over and closed his eyes and tenderly kissed Roni on the mouth. For a moment it felt as though Roni was kissing him back, but then he felt the sting of her hand across his face.

They stared at each other for a few moments. Jason could still be heard coughing and, without a word, Roni ran in his direction. Ryan stood a few moments more, holding his cheek and grinning. "Oh yeah. It was worth it," proclaimed the unrepentant boy. Then he took off in Jason's direction as well.

Both Roni and Ryan reached the coughing boy at almost the same time. Jason stood still, looking at both of them. Then he fell.

"Jason!" Roni screamed and ran over to him. She picked up her friend's lifeless body and cradled him in her arms.

"Do something, Ryan!" she screamed. "Help him!"

Ryan froze. He was the science wiz, what should he do? Maybe CPR? He took Jason's body from Roni and laid it out on the grass. He started compressions. He felt Jason's ribs crack beneath his hands. Although he knew this was supposed to happen, feeling his brother's bones give way made him sick to his stomach. He continued to pump his heart for almost twenty minutes. When he could no longer go on, he wearily leaned back on his heels.

"I can't do it, Roni. He's... he's dead."

"No. He can't be!"

"He is! I can't fix him!"

"Then what good is all your stupid science knowledge if you can't use it to save your own brother! You want him to die! You have always been jealous of him!" Roni picked Jason's head up again and held him, rocking him back and forth. She was crying uncontrollably.

Ryan knew he had not been a good brother to Jason. Many times he had wished he was an only child. It looked like his wish had come true.

Lightning flashed across the sky. Rain began to fall. Ryan turned around and started running.

Running and not looking back.

CHAPTER ONE

The Homecoming Game

"Your eyes saw my unformed body; all the days ordained for me were written in your book before one of them came to be."

Psalm 139:16, NIV

Friday Night—4th October

It seemed as though all seven hundred residents of Gage City had turned out to see the high school football game. Most small towns in southwest Kansas had little more for entertainment. It was a chilly October evening; a cool mist had been coming down all day, but it had finally let up by the time the game was ready to begin. It was homecoming week, so the stadium was packed with fans.

Roni stood in a circle with her cheer squad.

"All right, ladies, this is our night! We are gonna show this crowd what the Lady Cardinals are made of. No matter what happens out on that field tonight, we are gonna cheer for our guys like they are at the Super Bowl, leading by 50 points! Right?!"

"Right!" yelled the girls.

"Ok, all hands in. Go, Cardinals, on three! One, two, three... Go, Cardinals!"

Just as the squad began to get in cheering formation, Jeni, one of Roni's twin sisters, ran up.

"Roni! It's an emergency!"

"What? The concession stand is out of Yoo-hoo? That would be an emergency," Roni laughed.

"No, that's not it! Listen, Roni," said Jeni. "Nobody can find Carmen anywhere. She's supposed to sing the National Anthem. Quick, Mrs Dean says you have to come now and sing, or it's going to be a disaster!"

Roni rolled her eyes. "What? Really? I thought the music program was trying to diversify. I mean, our new music teacher said it wasn't all about me. Remember? I gave up the singing of the National Anthem to other qualified singers, and I use that term loosely."

"Come on, Roni. Don't make me beg. Mrs Dean doesn't know what she's talking about. You're the best singer in the county, and everyone knows it." Jeni paused and then grinned. "You know you want to make her eat her words since she called you a diva."

Roni considered the pleasure of that prospect.

"Oh all right," she smiled back at Jeni. "I *am* the best. Aren't I?" She tossed her hair dramatically and spoke in her best southern belle accent.

"Let's go then!" squealed Jeni. She grabbed Roni's hand and started to run.

"Lord, please help me," Roni prayed silently.

Nobody would believe how nervous she really was—no matter how many times she sang this song. All the way to the announcer's box, Roni tried to clear her throat. She always made weird animal noises to warm up her vocal cords.

"Meow, woof, tweet-tweet, moo..."

"Alright, finish up your barnyard noises and get cranking!" yelled Jeni.

***

Roni sang beautifully. Afterwards she glowed as she walked by the music teacher.

"Thank you, Roni."

"No problem, Mrs Dean."

She winked at her twin sisters. Jeni and Juli smiled and high-fived her. Just then they overheard some of their classmates talking.

"That took forever!"

"What? Does she think she is on America's Got Talent or something?"

"Mrs Dean was right. What a Diva!"

"Roni, just turn around and walk away." Jeni took her sister by the shoulders and attempted to turn her away from the girls.

"Roni! Roni! I heard you sing! It was fabulous!" Zoei, their five-year-old sister, came rushing up.

Roni scooped her into her arms.

"Thanks, Zo Bear! Who's your favorite sister?" she asked as she began to tickle her sister's stomach.

"You are! You are, Roni!" squealed Zoei.

"Hey! What about us?" chimed in Jeni and Juli.

"You're my *bestest* twin sisters!"

"How sweet," said Carmen in a sarcastic tone. "All the little orphans are one happy family. Hey Roni, you still letting Zoei call you her sister? I would have thought you would be ready to drop your unlikely story and let her call you Mom by now."

"I'm sure we've said it before," said Jeni defensively, "but maybe you're too stupid to remember that Zoei isn't Roni's daughter. You saw our mother pregnant with her, so I don't know why you can't accept the truth."

"Well, it's true we saw Carol with a little extra weight, but Roni was going through her chubby stage at the same time. Oh wait! I mean Roni was starting her extra chubby stage then. Exactly when is that stage going to be over, Roni?" Carmen and her friends started laughing.

Jeni came unglued. "How dare you! You are not even... worthy to speak our mother's name!" She lunged forward at Carmen and her following of shallow companions.

Juli reached out and grabbed her sister by the back of her cheerleader uniform, just in time to stop Jeni's fist from coming into contact with Carmen's face.

"Wow! I guess that red hair is no joke!" said Lindsey, one of the girls who was with Carmen.

Carmen leaned in toward Roni and snarled, "You had better keep your little Ginger Twins under control or else." She turned and walked away with her cronies.

Juli looked at Jeni. "So what was your plan after you knocked Carmen out? And did you really say 'you are not worthy'? That's it, you're cutting back on all the Jane Austen movies."

Jeni had the hotter temper of the twin sisters. The two girls looked exactly alike, except that Jeni's eyes were green and Juli's were blue. Their red hair was the butt of most of the jokes that their classmates invented. They were both tall and slender, with creamy white skin and a few scattered freckles on their faces. Jeni liked to take out her frustrations on the basketball court and was secretly a lover of English literature. Juli was dedicated to her music. She could play almost any instrument she picked up.

The twins, like Roni, had been adopted by John and Carol Chambers. Carol had been unable to carry a baby past the first trimester. However, when Roni was fourteen, Carol became pregnant. And, with much care and bed rest, Zoei was born. Then last year tragedy had struck. The girls' father was killed while fighting a fire. A few months later, their mother died too. She had never recovered after their father's death. All the doctors would say was that she must have died of a broken heart.

Roni was seventeen when their parents died. The girls wanted to stay together and have their eldest sister take care of them; so Roni decided to drop out of school for a year in order to go through the legal system and get custody of her sisters. She figured she could come back the next year to finish high school.

The three sisters walked to the bleachers, where the students were watching the game. Sharleen Miller came over to Roni.

"Are you ok?" she looked at Roni with concern.

"I'm ok. Just trying to get myself back in cheer mode," the girl answered.

"Is there something I can do?"

"You have already done so much for us. Thank you," replied Roni, giving her adopted mother a hug.

"Come on, Zoei," said Sharleen. "Let's go find our seats. Mr Greg will be looking for us."

Roni watched Sharleen walk away with Zoei. Greg and Sharleen Miller had been a great support to the Chambers girls after the death of their parents. The families had always been close. The couple had helped Roni with the funeral arrangements and made sure the girls knew how to manage the money their parents had left them. Zoei had become very attached to the Millers since they had taken care of her so much over the last year.

***

"Only five more minutes till halftime," thought Roni. "Five minutes to show all those wannabe Barbie dolls that you don't have to look like a Dallas Cowboys Cheerleader to rock the house."

Roni had been a cheerleader since seventh grade. All she had ever wanted to do was prove she was just as good as her size-two cheer mates. So finally, after five years of cheering, she was captain of the squad. Being five foot three and 160lbs wasn't the usual recipe for selection as captain of the high school cheerleaders, but the new cheer sponsor had watched Roni closely during tryouts and cheer camp and decided to give her charge of the squad of twelve girls.

The half-time buzzer sounded and the principal called out over the speakers, "Okay, Gage City, it's time to welcome the Cardinal Cheerleaders!"

The crowd cheered without much enthusiasm. The football team was down by thirty points. They hadn't won a game in years, so the apathy was somewhat understandable.

"The girls have prepared a dance routine for you tonight. Mixed and choreographed by Captain Roni Chambers!"

Not only had the football team lost every game in the last five years, the previous cheer squads hadn't been exactly inspiring either. They had ended last year with only two cheerleaders. Roni was hoping to change all that. She looked up at the night sky. The stars were so bright, even with the stadium lights on.

"Mama, Daddy, I miss you," she thought as she held on to the crystal pendant on her necklace. Quickly she tucked it back in her uniform, as it was against school policy to wear jewelry during a game. As she laid her hand on her chest, she could feel the necklace charm beneath her uniform. It had been a gift from her parents, right before her father died, and she had never taken it off.

"I know I'm just dancing for school spirit, but maybe you can still help me do a great job?" she whispered. She hadn't realized it, but Jeni and Juli were standing on either side of her, holding their charms as well. They took her by the hand. When they turned around, they saw that even Zoei, who was seated in the stands, had her hand around her necklace. Something about these necklaces seemed to draw the girls together. It was as if they could feel each other's thoughts and, when they held them, a sense of comfort came over them.

Roni looked at both of her sisters and smiled. Then she turned to the rest of her squad.

"All right, ladies. Let's do this!" she shouted.

The music started. About 15 seconds into the program, the crowd was on its feet and going wild. They were so loud the cheerleaders could hardly hear the music. Roni's smile said everything. The squad was working as a team and they were doing great.

Halfway through the routine, the pain began. Roni felt tightness in her chest. It took her breath away but she pushed through, even though the pain intensified all the way to the end of the dance. Since the routine ended with all the girls lying on the ground, nobody noticed when Roni didn't get up.

The crowd was yelling and applauding loudly. The other cheerleaders jumped up and basked in their moment of triumph. Roni continued to lie on the ground, clutching her chest and the crystal around her neck, as though it could make the pain stop. She could feel her heart pounding in her ears. Then all was quiet.

A wave of peace swept over her body. It was like nothing she had ever experienced before. She looked around. She was floating among the stars. Her senses were heightened. She could smell love. Taste peace. Touch joy. She wondered if this was what pure happiness felt like. It was something only the Creator himself could have made.

"Am I dead?" thought Roni.

"For now," said a gentle voice in her head.

The voice startled her.

"What does that mean?"

"It means that you should be dead but I still have things for you to do."

"What things?" asked Roni.

"You'll see. Just trust me."

Suddenly a volt of pain enveloped her body. Once. Twice. Three times. Each time more intense than the last. Roni screamed on the inside. Her eyes flickered open for a moment. She looked up. Just before she blacked out again, she thought she saw someone she hadn't seen in years.

"Ryan?"

CHAPTER 2

My Brother's Keeper

"And the LORD said unto Cain, Where is Abel
thy brother? And he said, I know not:
Am I my brother's keeper?"

Genesis 4:9

Nine Years Earlier

"Ryan Allen Miller! You are such a bully!"

Roni was screaming at the top of her lungs. The nine-year-old was ready to be judge, jury and executioner to the much larger child. Although they were the same age, Ryan had already reached five feet while Roni was still scrambling for the four-foot line. Her brown eyes were wide as she took on her stronger opponent. Her long brown hair whipped around in the western Kansas wind. She had the look of a wild, untamed horse. The young girl fought with such passion and purpose that it made the boy even more joyful to keep her at arm's length.

"Come on, Rapunzel," taunted Ryan. "Just a few more inches and you've got me."

Ryan had his hand on Roni's forehead. He laughed as she kept wildly swinging her arms at him. Finally she stopped. She turned her face away from him. A tear was forming in the corner of her eye and she didn't want the boy to see it.

"Why do you always have to be so mean to Jason?" asked Roni.

"Why do you always have to be so nice to him?" Ryan darted back. "He's such a big baby. Always pretending to be sick. I'm dizzy. I can't breathe. My chest hurts. Blah, blah, blah! I know he does it just to get out of chores and get attention. Why don't you go find yourself some real girlfriends to play with, instead of always hanging out with my sissy brother?"

Roni and Jason had been very close all their lives. Even as a baby, Jason would cry until his mom put him in Roni's crib. The babies would snuggle up to each other until they were almost nose to nose. They would sleep for hours and hours like that. If they woke up and weren't hungry or needed their diapers changed, they would just lie in the crib, cooing at each other.

Jason and Roni's moms hated to separate them, so the babies spent a lot of time sleeping at each other's houses. When they were three, Roni taught Jason to walk. He started talking around age four. Being developmentally delayed and having a slightly enlarged heart, Jason's progress was slow; but Roni was always there for him and always patient.

Ryan, on the other hand, looked for every opportunity to tease and humiliate Jason. He was an advanced child, hitting all the developmental checkpoints early. He was walking and talking at seven months. He could read by age two. Since he was a wiz at math and science, the Gage City School was running out of things for him to do. He was very tall for his age, and some would say almost muscular for a nine-year-old. His curly blond hair and intense blue eyes made all the girls in the fourth grade swoon. Jason's brown hair and eyes, along with his small stature, were so contrasting to Ryan's trim, well-built physique that it was hard to believe they were twins.

"Not identical, obviously," Ryan would always point out in a superior sounding voice.

The Millers had adopted them when they were just a few days old. It was quite apparent from the beginning that they weren't identical. Jason was small and needy, while Ryan was a strong, independent boy. The problem had always been that, while Jason needed most of his parents' attention, Ryan wanted it all.

Ryan would go out of his way to put on a good show of strength and intelligence, which mesmerized his classmates but was growing increasingly aggravating to his teachers. Jason was so very good-natured that all the adults who knew him had a special place in their heart for him. This, of course, angered Ryan.

One day Ryan was feeling particularly irritated with his brother. Jason had just gotten over another bout of pneumonia and was returning to school after being away for almost a month. All morning the teachers had been welcoming him back and telling him how much they missed him, and Roni was there holding his hand as usual. She wouldn't let him get more than a yard away from her.

Ryan watched this the whole morning. He was getting so furious that his ears were turning red. After lunch, when all the children were at the playground, he began to hatch his plan. It had been raining the last few days, so there were puddles of standing water scattered around the playground. One particularly large one, over by the teeter totters, caught Ryan's eye. There were butterflies and dragonflies hovering over the water.

"Hey, Roni," he called over to her. "You should come over and see these butterflies."

"She can't resist butterflies," he said to himself.

Roni walked warily over to the puddle. To her delight, there were a lot of butterflies. Yellow and orange and green ones. A little purple one flew right in front of her face. It landed on her nose for a few moments. She was so elated that she let go of Jason's hand and marveled at the exquisite creature. The butterfly stuck out its proboscis and it looked as though it was licking her.

She giggled, "Look Ja..."

SPLASH!!!

Roni came out of her trance, and there was Jason sitting in the puddle, wiping rainwater out of his eyes.

"What happened?" asked Roni as she stooped to help the wet boy out of the water.

Jason was soaked from head to toe. She heard a suppressed laugh behind her and turned around. One look at Ryan's face and she knew he was the culprit. She lunged toward the devious boy.

"Ryan Allen Miller! You are such a bully!"

"Come on, Rapunzel. Just a few more inches and you've got me!"

"Why do you have to be so mean to Jason?"

"Why do you have to be so nice to him?"

Ryan continued on, but Roni wasn't listening. She turned away and finished helping Jason out of the puddle and onto dry ground.

"Why don't you go find yourself some real girlfriends to play with, instead of hanging out with my sissy brother?"

Roni turned back and faced Ryan. Before he had time to say anything else, she kicked him hard in the shin.

"I pick my own friends, thank you," she said.

The boy had reached over to grab his throbbing shin, and Roni decided to take another moment to reemphasize her point. She pushed him back on his rear end and put her forehead onto his. She looked directly into his eyes.

"And don't call me Rapunzel!"

CHAPTER 3

Rapunzel Revived

*"But God will redeem me from the realm of the dead;
he will surely take me to himself."*

Psalm 49:15, NIV

Wednesday 9ᵗʰ October

"Rapunzel... Rapunzel.... Roni, wake up... Roni... Roni..."

Roni could hear her name being called, but she couldn't respond. Her eyes felt heavy. Her throat hurt. She tried to clear it.

"No, no... wait, Roni. Let me get... wait. Roni... wait!"

Then she felt it. A searing pain in and on her chest. It felt like someone had opened her chest, pulled out her heart, kicked it around like a soccer ball, and shoved it back in her. She wondered if she had been sewn up with a needle the size of a train track spike. She began pulling at her tubes and monitors, thrashing around in a panic to break free of her torturers.

"No, Roni. Stop! No one wants to hurt you!"

She could hear beeping and buzzing all around, like the tones going off at her father's firehouse when there was a particularly large fire for them all to handle. Roni tried hard to scream but no sound was coming out. The pain in her chest grew more and more excruciating. She was being held down on all sides. Then she heard a long flat tone and she was out again...

The next sound she could hear... it seemed like a long while later... was a whisper.

"Oh God, please give me the wisdom to know how to save her. I've already failed her in so many ways. Please help me."

***

"How many days has she been like this, Doctor?" asked an inquisitive first-year medical student.

"This is her eighth day since she tried to pull everything out. I told the nurses and CNAs not to try to wake her. I need to be here in case she panics again," replied the doctor.

"Isn't it taking her a long time to come around?" asked a second student.

"She has had open heart surgery three times in the last two weeks. She is also on her second pacemaker. Rest seems to be the thing to prescribe in this case."

"Dr Miller, why are you going through so much trouble for one patient? It would seem reasonable to have given up over a week ago."

"She's special," replied Ryan.

CHAPTER 4

"I Will Be There for You"

"Yea, though I walk through the valley of the shadow of death, I will fear no evil: for thou art with me."

Psalm 23:4a

Saturday 19th October

Roni could feel the warmth of sunlight on her face. The air smelled like a meadow full of flowers. She stretched her hands out slowly to feel the grass, but the ground felt more like... a blanket. When she moved her head, it became obvious to her that she was in a bed, but it wasn't hers. And, for some reason, the top of her hand and the middle of her back were aching more than the rest of her body.

She slowly opened her eyes. The light hurt... as if she hadn't seen daylight for a long time. When the blurriness was gone, she saw that she was in a white room and the pain on her hand was from an IV. She figured she must be in a hospital. There were vases and baskets of flowers everywhere. Several bouquets of balloons were on the floor next to her bed.

A teddy bear with a Cardinal Cheerleader outfit sat next to a lamp at the foot of her bed. Beside it was a recliner, and in the recliner sat a young doctor. He was fast asleep. He looked as though he hadn't changed his clothes in days, and he was in desperate need of a shave. Roni looked at the physician closely. There was something familiar about him. He had curly blond hair and resembled Chris Hemsworth.

"Maybe I've died, and gone to heaven, and Chris Hemsworth is my doctor," she smiled at the delightful thought.

A nurse entered the room and, seeing that Roni was awake, she walked over to the chair. She put her hand on the doctor's shoulder and shook him a little.

"Dr Miller. Dr Miller. Your patient is awake."

Ryan awoke with a start. "Oh yes... um... ok."

He jumped up from his seat and dropped his stethoscope on the floor. He reached down quickly to pick it up. When he leaned over, two pens and a small notebook fell out of his shirt pocket. He clumsily retrieved his property.

Roni giggled at the sight of the disheveled doctor, but the slight movement brought on a spasm of pain.

"Ouch!" she yelped. "Oh... oh... oh!" She cried and reached for her necklace, but it wasn't there.

Ryan jumped up and was at her bedside in a flash. "It's ok, Roni. Here's your necklace," and he placed it in her hand. She immediately felt some relief.

"You're okay. Just breathe slowly. Gayle, get me some pain meds for her. Slowly, Roni. In and out."

"What do you want me to get her, Doctor?" asked the nurse frantically.

Ryan, looking rather annoyed at the nurse, said, "Check her chart. Slow down your breathing, Roni, or you're going to hyperventilate."

She did the best she could. The nurse got the pain meds in her and she began to feel much better. Ryan helped her for about half an hour, until her pain was managed and her breathing under control.

"I want you to try and eat something, Roni," the doctor said. "Just a little bit. You haven't had solid food for over two weeks, maybe some Jell-O? I have to get a shower and see some of my other patients, but I will be back to talk to you. I'll be as quick as I can."

"Ok. Just as long as it's not green Jell-O," she said with a smile.

Ryan smiled back. "Got it, Rapunzel."

***

"Green Jell-O, ugh!" thought Roni to herself. "Is there no justice in this world? I'm only eighteen years old. I've had a heart attack. I have a mini electric chair keeping my heart going, and now this. Green Jell-O. Could life get any worse?"

Roni pulled down the collar of her hospital gown and looked at her chest. She gently touched the delicate stitches and large staples that were keeping her skin together. She traced the outline of the pacemaker with her finger. Her heart was beating strong. Aside from the stitches on her chest, there was a lot of bruising on her arms, breast and stomach.

A nurse named Priscilla, who came in to check on her, said the doctor had gone overboard to save her. She should have been dead, but he kept on trying to save her when most doctors would have let her die.

"I was there in the operating room that third and last time when he held your heart in his hands," said the nurse. "He was weeping and praying that it would beat again. I've been in several open heart procedures with Dr Miller, and I have never seen him in such a state.

21

"Then it was almost miraculous. As soon as he'd finished praying, your heart began to pump, right there in his hands. He stayed to the end of each of your surgeries. He even stitched you up himself."

Priscilla began to laugh. "Some of the nurses had to go to his house and bring the doctor clean clothes and his comb and toothbrush. He hasn't left the hospital in over two weeks. He's beginning to look like one of those Duck Dynasty brothers!"

Roni laughed a little but was careful not to agitate her stitches.

"You're just lucky Dr Miller happened to be at that football game, or you would be cheering for St Peter at the pearly gates right now," Priscilla continued. "Well, I'm done here. You press the call button for the nurse, if you need to go to the bathroom or if you get to hurting bad again. Bye-bye, sweetheart."

She kissed Roni on the head and left. That was a little strange for a nurse, but Roni didn't mind. It had been a good long time since she had been mothered. It was nice. She began to think about what Priscilla had said about Ryan saving her and having her heart in his hands. Her mind went back to that last time she had seen him, when they were twelve. The night Jason died. That night when neither one of them could save him, no matter how hard they tried.

She wiped a tear from her eye. She hadn't seen Ryan since that night, and now he just happened to show up when she had a heart attack. Strange. *And how is it that he is not only a doctor but a heart surgeon too? We are only eighteen years old. I knew he was smart, but wow!*

She was beginning to feel sleepy again. The medication the nurse brought with her green Jell-O was starting to take effect.

"Where is Ryan?" she thought. "He said he'd be back soon."

She looked out the window. The sun was beginning to set. She thought about her sisters and wondered if they were safe. She touched her necklace.

"I hope they know that I'm ok."

Roni's eyes slowly began to shut. She was feeling very relaxed. Suddenly she opened her eyes and sat up in bed. "Oh no!" she said out loud. Something worse than green Jell-O had just occurred to her.

"Ryan saw me naked!"

***

Ryan sat on the edge of Roni's bed. He reached over and brushed a strand of hair out of her face. Her long hair was pulled over to one side. Ryan had always loved to look at her hair. It was like a waterfall cascading down her back. When the sun shone on it, it glowed, and he thought she looked like an angel. He had even nicknamed her Rapunzel. Unfortunately, his behavior had made her hate that name.

He had loved Roni since they were children, but Jason had always come between them. When his brother died, Ryan could no longer face her. So he begged his parents to send him away to an overseas boarding school. Several schools had sent acceptance letters to him. He left for Germany the next morning; there, he finished junior high in three months and high school six months later.

After that, he immediately started medical school and went into cardiovascular studies. He hoped that, by going into the medical profession and helping people, he might somehow atone for what had happened with Jason. Seeing his parents at the game a few weeks ago had stirred his tormented soul anew.

Roni began to stir as Ryan stroked her hair.

"Roni? Roni? Are you awake?" he whispered.

"Not yet," she replied.

"Are you thirsty?" asked Ryan. "I've got some water and a Yoo-hoo for you."

"Yoo-hoo?" she said without even opening her eyes. "I love Yoo-hoo."

"I know," he smiled. "Want me to raise your bed up a bit so you can get a drink?"

"Yes, please," she replied.

He pushed the *up* button on her bed. She finally opened her eyes and looked at him. They stared intently at each other until the bed was in the upright position.

"Oh... ah... here you go." He held the straw up to her mouth. She drank the Yoo-hoo slowly. He had never forgotten the perfection of her face.

"So... um... how have you been?" stammered Ryan.

Roni looked up at him curiously. "Well... I've just had a heart attack, and an eighteen-year-old doctor cut me open and stuck a nine-volt battery in my chest. Oh, and the doctor is my best friend's brother, who used to torment me as a kid, AND he has seen me naked. Thanks for asking. How have you been?"

Ryan's face turned red.

"Uhh... fine... I guess. Guess that was kind of a silly question."

"You think? So give me the rundown on what's wrong with me," said Roni, changing the subject.

"Well," began Ryan, "You haven't had a heart attack; you have gone into cardiac arrest several times in the last few weeks. Basically the electrical current, that keeps your heart going, quit. I've had to put a specially made pacemaker in you to keep your heart from stopping. It's much larger than a regular one, but a regular-size one wouldn't do the job. You will have to take a special medication in order to keep your body from attacking the pacemaker."

Roni stared at Ryan dumbfounded. She was still having a hard time accepting that her heart had given out on her in the first place. *And now she was going to have to be on medication for the rest of her life?*

"What does that mean?" Roni asked, her lips quivering. "Will I have to stay in bed for the rest of my life?" A tear slid down her cheek.

"No, no!" said Ryan, and he put his arm around her. "You won't have to stay in bed. You will have a regular life, for the most part."

Roni was an emotional wreck. She started sobbing. Ryan held her close, stroking her hair.

"Roni, you have a long road to recovery, but I promise I will be there for you every step of the way. Don't worry. I won't leave you alone."

CHAPTER 5

AIRborn Secrets

*"My flesh and my heart faileth: but God is the strength
of my heart, and my portion forever."*

Psalm 73:26

Sunday 20th October—Thursday 31st October

Over the next few weeks, Ryan was true to his word. He
kept his promise to Roni and helped her through the long,
grueling recovery process. They had dinner together
almost every night. The hospital food could get a little
tasteless, so he would sneak pizza and Yoo-hoo in to her.

"You're not helping me fit back into my cheer
uniform," she would tease, knowing full well that she
would probably never cheer again.

Talking with Ryan made her laugh like she used to
when they were younger. Like when they spent their
summers at the lake. The lake where Jason had died. Her
family had not been back there since that sad night. Roni
tried not to think about Jason while she was trying to
recover. She just wanted to pretend that she and Ryan had
always been great friends.

The medication she had to take came in the form of
shots. The needles burned going into the already bruised
skin on her chest. Roni tried to be brave and hold back her
tears. At least she only needed them once a week instead
of every day.

Ryan made sure she had the best physical therapists
to help her regain her strength. Twice a day, she would go
down to the physical therapy room to work out. Ryan was
there as often as he could. Stretching each muscle and

tendon was harder and more painful than it sounded, and Roni would cry out when the pain got too much. Ryan encouraged her to persevere. He had unknowingly begun to cheer her on, as she had once done for Jason.

Since Roni's transfer to the hospital in Wichita, Zoei had stayed with the Millers. She and the twins drove up every weekend to see Roni. Greg and Sharleen came with them as well. They hoped to be reunited with their son, but Ryan was always too busy to sit and talk for long. He still felt guilty about his behavior when his brother died, and enjoying his parents seemed like a privilege he didn't deserve.

The sisters missed each other terribly. Whenever it was time for the twins and Zoei to go home, tears would flow. After the fourth weekend, Roni asked Ryan if they could talk.

"I've got some questions I've wanted to ask you," she began. "I need some answers. You still haven't told me how my heart could just stop. Why do I need a pacemaker? Why do I need all these shots? What does the medication do? How come you were at the football game? And more importantly where have you been and how is it that you are a heart surgeon and..."

"Stop, stop, stop!" laughed Ryan. "I will answer all your questions but only one at a time. Prioritize, please!"

"I'm serious, Ryan. I need answers."

"Ok. How about I start at the beginning? But you can't interrupt me until I've finished."

"Ok," agreed Roni.

"The night Jason died..." Ryan choked a bit. "The night Jason died I planned never to see you again. I had been such a jerk when we were all growing up, and then he died. I felt like it was my fault. I know now it wasn't, but I could have been a much better brother while he was still alive. I left for Germany the next day. A school out there had been trying to get me to come and finish my education at their facility.

"I knew Jason had died from complications relating to heart failure. A blood clot got knocked loose from somewhere in his body and went to his heart. I decided to go into cardiac medicine to somehow make up for being such a terrible brother. I was curious to know why Jason had a bad heart and I was so healthy; so I started by trying to find some information about our parents, in an effort to piece together a family medical history.

"My mom told me they had adopted us through a private adoption agency that found homes for orphans living in Russia. It was called AIRborn Adoptions. Both your parents and mine had used them. You remember our moms told us how we all arrived in Gage City on the same night? I looked and looked for the orphanage and adoption agency all over Russia, but I came up empty-handed.

"Then one day, about a year ago, I came across a business called AIRborn Industries. It was a computer technology research facility, supposedly located in a federal subject of Russia called Krasnoyarsk Krai. Most of the territory, or krai as they call it, is located in the middle of Siberia. I decided to go to the city of Krasnoyarsk. When I got there, I discovered that Krasnoyarsk City had never had any businesses of any kind called AIRborn.

"I was beginning to feel hopeless. Then one day, while sitting in a library in Krasnoyarsk City, a man came and sat next to me. He said his name was Michael, and he knew what I was looking for and he could help me find it.

I was alarmed and was wondering how long the KGB had been following me. Well, it turned out that Michael wasn't KGB. He was in fact not even close to anything I could have imagined. But I'm jumping ahead.

"We left the next morning to go to a city in northern Krasnoyarsk called Norilsk. It was located on the edge of a lava formation called the Siberian Traps. It was originally a slave mining camp. The pollution there is so bad the average lifespan is ten years shorter than in any other part of Russia. The mortality rate for children is high in Norilsk because of respiratory infections. Norilsk Nickel is the factory responsible for the pollution. The plants were built in the Soviet Era, a period when environmental controls didn't exist. In America we wouldn't consider this a place to settle down and raise a family.

"One thing of interest Norilsk had for us, though, was a small shop business called AIRborn Industries. We knocked on the door, but it was clear from the outside of the building that it had been uninhabited for a long time. We found the owner, Janes (Yanez), who said the shop had been abandoned about ten years back. He thought the occupants had had some legal trouble or something. He let us look around, for a price, which we didn't mind paying. The city is so poor. Everyone looked like they could use a handout.

"We spent about a week going through boxes and boxes of documents and papers we found in the shop. People heard that I was a doctor, so they brought me all kinds of free business. I did all I could. My best piece of medical advice was—MOVE!" Ryan laughed at his own sad attempt at humor. Roni wasn't amused.

Ryan continued, "Then Janes came in one day and said someone in town had snitched, and he was expecting some military people to show up any day. We had sorted out a few piles of official-looking papers and what looked like medical research. We boxed them up that night and took them to the basement in Janes' house. He let us hide out there for a few days until the military people had gone. They of course torched the shop with the rest of its contents before they left.

"The town was sorry to see us go, but we didn't want to endanger their lives. The people were so thankful for the medical care I had provided that they gave us enough provisions for ten people when we left. We were able to get some of the research and documents copied on a digital camera but we ran out of memory cards, so Janes arranged for the boxes to be mailed to several addresses here in the US. In fact, there are probably some strange-looking packages back in Gage City waiting for me right now. It was about six months ago when we left."

Ryan stopped for a moment to get a drink.

"You haven't told me how you happened to be at the football game," said Roni.

"Ya, I'm getting to that," said Ryan. "That fortunate meeting has to do with Michael. But let me go back to where I left off. I got back to Germany. Michael said he had some stuff to do, so he would try to catch up with me in a few weeks. I began to pick apart and translate some of the research I had copied from Norilsk. I discovered that someone had been trying to construct what looked like a super pacemaker. I began my own version of the machine right away. It was a little slow-going because a lot of the papers had been damaged by dust and mildew.

Plus, I was a little rusty on the dialect of Russian the research was written in."

Roni interrupted Ryan. "You should have shown it to Jeni. I swear that girl can figure out any language."

"Interesting..." said Ryan. He was silent for a moment.

"Ryan? You ok?"

"Yes... um, yes. Anyway, I figured out one reason the research was being done in nowheresville Russia. In 1908 a meteorite had exploded in midair near Norilsk, levelling a lot of trees on the Siberian Traps and depositing high amounts of iridium in the area. The scientists were attempting to use the iridium in making their super pacemaker. One thing I still couldn't understand, though, was why they needed to make a super pacemaker, unless they were trying to put one in an elephant or a dinosaur.

"I transferred back to the US, to a heart research facility in Wichita. In exchange for my services, they let me work on my super pacemaker.

"I sent another scientist to Norilsk to get some of the iridium. Janes managed to get him near ground zero of the meteorite explosion. They were able to get me about half an ounce of the element."

"That's it?" asked Roni.

"That's a lot. One ounce of the stuff costs almost nine hundred dollars."

"Oh. I see. Did you ever find out why they needed to make the super pacemaker?"

"I did," answered Ryan, and then he looked down at his feet. He hesitated. "Well... I discovered that certain hearts, like yours, not only need pacemakers to help make sure your heart keeps beating but... um... the pacemakers also need to be... protected from being attacked."

"Like people who get organ transplants and need anti-rejection medication?" asked Roni.

"Sort of," Ryan replied nervously. "Your case is a bit more complicated than that."

"How is it more complicated?" she said slowly, with a puzzled look on her face.

"Well," said Ryan. He paused for a few moments.

"There is... ah... something... living in you... that will attack any foreign object introduced into your body."

"Living? In me? Well, what is it?" asked Roni. Her voice cracked.

"Roni, do you know what nanotechnology is?"

Her face began to turn white as fear welled up in the back of her throat. "Yes," she whispered.

"While I was translating the research, I found out what the A-I-R in AIRborn stands for. It's an acronym for Artificial Intelligence Robotics.

"It seems that you have nanites, little robots, in your blood stream... possibly in other systems of your body, but your blood for sure. When I put the first pacemaker in, the nanites in your body attacked and destroyed it. I had been working on my super pacemaker for the last six months, so I thought I'd give it a go in you. I had nothing to lose."

"Nothing?" said Roni, as her eyes filled to the brim with tears.

"Nothing... except you," Ryan replied. His eyes began to glisten and he moved closer to his anxious friend.

"I did everything I could to save you and more," He said, pulling her close to him. She laid her head on his chest.

"I... I love you, Roni," he whispered, almost to himself. "I always have."

CHAPTER 6

Mr Hot Finger

"Amazing grace! How sweet the sound
That saved a wretch like me!
I once was lost, but now am found;
Was blind, but now I see."

From the hymn *"Amazing Grace"* by John Newton

Friday 1st November

Later the next day, after Ryan got off work, he decided to take Roni out for a walk in the hospital gardens. It was cold outside. Hardly any flowers were in bloom except for some mums and a few purple and yellow pansies that dotted the landscape. Ryan had brought a wheelchair with a lot of extra blankets. He lifted Roni gently from the bed and carried her over to the chair. She marveled at his strength. Most boys couldn't lift her without putting in a lot of effort, but he carried her as if she weighed nothing at all.

She found herself staring at his face as he tucked her in tightly but carefully. Those eyes, like pools of deep blue water, could pierce your soul. His hair was still just a mass of untamed, golden curls. When they were children, it used to grow so long during the summertime it almost reached his shoulders. Once, when Roni, Jason and Ryan were ten and they were lying on the beach after a long swim, she had reached over to Ryan and touched his hair. It was soft like silk. Ryan had pretended to be asleep then, but he never forgot that moment.

Though his face seemed like that of a man, Roni could still see in him the boy she remembered. His brow was furrowed, like it was that last night when they had tried to revive Jason. When they could do no more for him, Ryan had run away and left her there, holding Jason's lifeless body. She began to wonder at what point he would abandon her now. Suddenly Ryan interrupted her thoughts.

"I have something for you," he said, flashing his charming smile.

He presented her with a pair of zebra-striped slipper boots and a hat to match.

Roni laughed as she put the hat on.

"Thanks. Am I ready to take a trek out into the Siberian Flats?" she asked.

"Traps, Siberian Traps," said Ryan. "And no, the clothing you need to survive out there isn't available in Kansas."

He slipped the boots onto her feet. "Maybe I should call you Cinderella from now on."

Roni smiled and rolled her eyes.

The cold air outside was a refreshing change from the stuffy halls and rooms in the hospital. Roni breathed in deeply. She looked about the grounds and wished it were spring. She could see where the roses would be in bloom and wondered what color they were. There were a couple of Canada geese wandering around a pond that was just about to freeze over. The fountain had been turned off and the whole place seemed somewhat desolate. After about twenty minutes, Ryan suggested that they go back inside. He wasn't as bundled up as she was, and she could see that he was really beginning to feel the cold. They went back to Roni's room and Ryan unbundled her.

"I'm going to take a look at your incision, Roni. I know I've been letting the nurses do it but, as your doctor, I really need to see it myself. I promise that I'll try to make it as quick and emotionally painless as possible."

He ended his sentence abruptly, turned around and left. Roni wasn't sure if he was just still cold but she thought she saw his face turning a little red.

"Well, at least it's going to be as awkward for him as it is for me," she consoled herself.

***

Ryan tried not to look Roni in the eye while he was checking her incisions. All the places where her tubes and monitors had been were healing nicely. Most of her bruising had gone down. Roni knew that the scars on her chest would never go away. She had always been proud of her perfect, unblemished skin. Now her vanity had been squelched a little.

"All right then," said Ryan as he covered her up. "I want to check something on your back. Would you sit up, please, and face the door?"

Roni swung her legs around to the side of the bed. She leaned forward. Ryan ran his hand down her spine.

"Now I'm going to apply some pressure right here and I want you to tell me how you feel."

He pushed a little.

"How does that feel?"

"Fine."

"How about here?"

"Fine too."

He felt around for another ten minutes.

"Are you a chiropractor now, Ryan?" she laughed.

"Very funny, ha, ha," he replied. "I'm going to push a little harder right here. Tell me how this fee..."

Roni screamed out in agony. She fell back on the bed. Her body was rigid and she was gasping for breath.

"Roni, Roni, look at me! Roni, please look at me!" Ryan yelled at her. He tried desperately to make eye contact. "Roni."

She began to relax a bit as she concentrated on his voice. He turned her body and laid her head on a pillow. He stroked her hair and spoke softly until she was completely calm. She reached up and put her hand on the back of his neck and pulled his face close to her.

"I... I... uh... I think I might have... felt something there," she whispered.

He pulled away and saw her smile slightly. Then she fell asleep.

***

Sunday 3rd November

Sunlight appeared suddenly and Roni could hear a familiar voice.

"Good morning, sleepyhead! It's a beautiful day. Time to get up and enjoy it."

It was Priscilla. It had been two days since Ryan examined her back, and she had slept most of both days. Her back ached a bit in the trigger spot.

"It's Sunday and your sisters are coming today. A little birdie told me that you might be going home very soon. That's sure a reason to rejoice. Tell me how have you been since the last time we talked?"

"Well," said Roni. "I've got some weird robot bugs in me that don't want my heart to run, and I might be crushing on my childhood bully."

Priscilla laughed out loud. "Ha, ha, ha! The Lord works in mysterious ways."

"What does the Lord have to do with it?" asked Roni.

"For a beautiful princess like you to fall in love with her dragon, the Lord would have to be involved," said Priscilla. "Ah, love. Love is the Creator's ultimate gift to mankind. And, speaking of gifts, it's been a long time since I heard that angelic voice of yours. How about singing 'Amazing Grace'? We can do a duet."

"Oh... well, I don't know. It's been a while..."

Roni started to make excuses and wondered how this nurse knew that she could sing.

"Oh come on, baby, you've got to use the gifts the Lord gave you."

"Ok," Roni agreed reluctantly.

Ryan had just finished his rounds and was about to come into the room when he heard Roni singing.

"Amazing grace! How sweet the sound that saved a wretch like me! I once was lost, but now am found; was blind, but now I see."

Roni and Priscilla sang as many verses of "Amazing Grace" as they could think of. On the last verse, Roni looked out the window in her room at the rising sun. The beauty of the dawn was reflected in her voice. It had snowed overnight and the world looked like an Ansel Adams photograph. Frost covered every branch of every tree and the whole landscape sparkled in the rays of the new day.

Suddenly a Cardinal landed on the sill of Roni's window, and she marveled at the creature's splendor. Its brilliant red feathers made it look like a Christmas tree ornament. It appeared as though the ruby feathered bird was singing along with the two women as it opened and closed its beak. It fluttered its wings and its chest vibrated as the sound echoed from its small mouth. Although the bird was on the other side of a window over an inch thick, Roni could somehow hear its beautiful song.

When the song was finished, Roni turned around expecting to see Priscilla; but instead she saw Ryan and about half a dozen interns and nurses. They were standing there with their mouths open, amazed by what they had just heard.

"Oh, I'm sorry," she stammered. "I was just... singing... I mean, we were singing and I... sometimes get carried away... Um, where did the nurse go?"

"I didn't see a nurse. She must have left before I got here," said Ryan.

"Oh, well, she was just here."

"I forgot how intoxicating your voice was... is."

The other people left, while Ryan stood there. Frozen.

"Oh. Um. Thank you," murmured Roni.

There was an awkward silence. Ryan finally found his voice. "I wanted to talk to you some more about the research I found in Norilsk. Can I look at your back again?"

Roni's forehead wrinkled up. It was obvious that she was frightened by the prospect of more pain. Ryan tried to reassure her that he wouldn't hurt her again. She finally agreed—reluctantly—to his request. He looked at the place where he had applied intolerable pressure just two days ago. In the center of her back, an inky spot had appeared where his thumb had been. Raised veins emanated about three inches from the dark blotch.

"I want to take a picture of this," said Ryan.

"What! What is it?" cried Roni, alarmed.

"It's just a bruise. Don't worry," he reassured her with a smile and then left to get a camera.

Roni sat on her bed, waiting for Ryan. He had been gone a while, so she pulled on her hospital housecoat and walked over to the window. The sun was warming the air outside, causing the frost to melt and turning the hospital garden into a rainbow of shimmering crystal.

The little red bird was still perched on the windowsill. It propelled itself off the window ledge and hovered in front of Roni's face. A shrill sound was coming from its beak and she thought the tiny bird was trying to tell her something. Skeptically she strained her ear, trying to decipher the sounds it was making. When she felt a hand on her shoulder, she began to feel a little foolish. Thinking it was Ryan, she backed away from the glass and put her hand on his.

"It's a beautiful day, isn't it?" she said.

"It certainly is," said a voice behind her.

Roni wheeled around to find a stranger in a scarlet jacket standing behind her. She let out a small scream.

"Who are you?" she asked in a frightened voice and backed into the corner of her room. Her eyes darted wildly from one side of the room to the other. There was no escape. She wanted to scream but no sound would come out of her mouth.

"I am sorry," the stranger spoke in a smooth voice. "I did not mean to alarm you." He took a step closer to her.

"I am Mr Ezekiel. I mean you no harm."

The man standing before Roni was tall, with black hair. A sharp, pointed nose was set above his full lips, which were unnaturally red. His eyes were black as coal and hypnotic to the point of lulling one into obedience. The shoes on his feet looked as though he had walked through the snow and not even bothered to shake it off when he came inside. He was leaving a puddle where he stood.

"What do you want?" Roni could get barely more than a whisper out.

"Only to help you." He took two more steps toward her. "I heard of your terrible affliction. The person I work for is very interested in helping you. There is no reason for you to suffer all the pain and disfigurement of such a large, bulky machine inside your chest."

Roni put her hand over her heart. How did this man know about her? She started shaking.

"And that scar."

He continued to walk forward as he removed one of his black gloves. He stopped only when he was close enough to touch her.

"What a shame to blemish such... perfect skin."

He put his finger on her cheek softly. At first his finger felt icy cold but within seconds it had turned white hot. Roni screamed out as he held his finger steadily in one place on her cheek. He seemed to relish seeing her in pain. Tears ran down her face. She was in a state of utter torment.

"You will submit to me, my daughter," his voice echoed in her head.

When she felt like she could bear no more, she heard a familiar voice.

"In the name of the Lord of hosts, leave here!"

A rush of hot wind filled the room, blasting what felt like sand on Roni's face. She collapsed. Then the room was as it had been before.

"Oh baby, come here. What has that demon done to you? You are safe now."

Roni opened her eyes. It was Priscilla; she held Roni in her arms and rocked her.

"He's gone. He can't hurt you anymore," Priscilla was weeping now. "I only turned my back for a moment and the enemy pounced. I didn't know he knew where you were. I thought we had hidden you well enough. I will never leave you alone again, Roni. I promise."

The next thing she knew, Ryan came rushing into the room.

"Roni, are you ok?"

Roni opened her eyes. She was in her bed again. Not sure if she had just dreamt up Ezekiel, she put her hand on her face. The place where he had touched her was still hot. She looked down at the floor and the puddle of melted snow was still there.

"Ryan? There was a man here... He... he... knew stuff about me. He hurt my face. Then... she... Priscilla came... and how did I get in my bed? She couldn't possibly have lifted me."

"It's ok. I'm here. Michael is here. We have to move you to a safer place."

"Safer place? What?" Roni's head was beginning to clear. "We should call the police."

"The police can't help us, Roni. Only Michael can."

"You mean the guy that just walked up to you in the Russian library who isn't the KGB? What does he have to do with any of this? How can he help? Ryan, what's going on?!" Roni was getting frantic. She jumped out of bed. She was still a little wobbly on her legs and had to lean back on the edge of her bed to steady herself.

"Let me get you safe, and then I will explain everything. I promise." Ryan grabbed a plastic bag out of the closet and began throwing her stuff in it.

"Here, put this on." He tossed her a pair of jeans and a grey Cardinal t-shirt. She examined the clothes for a few seconds, then made her way over to him.

"Stop, Ryan, stop! I'm not doing anything until you tell me what's going on!"

He was holding her medical chart and another clipboard, trying to fill out her discharge papers and commit to memory any medications she might need.

"Roni, just get dressed!" he said, without looking up at her. She knocked the clipboard and medical chart from his hands and grabbed him by the shoulders, clutching his shirt to keep from falling.

"No! Not until you tell me something. Who is Michael and why are you so bent on listening to him? How do you know he isn't with Mr... Hot Finger? Ryan!"

They were standing toe to toe, neither willing to budge an inch. It was like they were twelve years old again, standing alone in the woods. Ryan's arms were holding her close. For a moment he lost his sense of purpose and leaned his head towards her. The desire to relive the one and only kiss they had ever shared seemed to overcome him. Time stood still, and Roni leaned her head in, as if she too craved his lips on hers. Breathing in her scent was intoxicating. He moved in a little closer, savoring her essence. He was so close he could feel her breath on his mouth.

A loud beeping sound brought Ryan back to his senses. It was Roni's oxygen monitor. It had come off her finger when she jumped out of bed. A nurse came into the room but turned and left when she saw that everything was under control. Ryan backed away and retrieved his clipboards.

Roni was leaning against the bed once again. Her flushed face betrayed her heart.

"You won't believe me if I just blurt it out."

"Try me," said Roni.

"I'm telling you, you won't..."

"Try me, Ryan, and quit dancing around!" Roni yelled out in desperation.

"Fine. You want me to quit dancing?" he hollered back.

"Yes!" roared Roni.

"Ok, Princess. Michael was the one who told me your heart was going to quit. That's how come I was in Gage City that night. He was the one who kept us from falling into the hands of the soldiers in Norilsk. Michael was the one who told me to hightail it down here because something was wrong. He knew you were in danger."

Roni frowned at him. "How does he know all this?"

"It's because he.... It's because he's an... It's..."

Ryan was stammering. He couldn't believe he was going to tell her this important piece of information like this. He had practiced and practiced how he was going to say it just right, so Roni wouldn't think he was crazy.

"He's what, Ryan?"

"He's an angel."

CHAPTER 7

Angels on Alert

*"I cry out to God Most High, to God who will
fulfill his purpose for me."*

Psalm 57:2, NLT

Roni sat in the passenger seat of Ryan's car, staring ahead in disbelief at the information she had just heard.

"An angel? Really?" she thought to herself. "Why would Ryan make up such a ridiculous story? Why did he whisk me away so secretly from the hospital like that? What about my sisters? They are coming today!"

"Roni, are you all right?" Ryan tried to get her attention. "Roni, I'm sorry I had to tell you like that. I know it's hard to believe but..."

"What about my sisters?" she interrupted him. "They are coming to see me today."

"I've already called my parents and Michael has gone on to protect the girls. He says he has another... um... friend to help him."

He added the last part reluctantly as he wasn't sure how much Roni believed of what he had told her. "He will bring them to your parents' old lake house tomorrow."

"The lake house? A friend? What, another angel? Ryan, if this is some savior complex you have developed because you think it will make up for leaving me with Jason, you are mistaken. You can't make up for that. There are no do-overs in life!"

There was a long period of silence. It was seventy-five miles to the lake house from the hospital, so they had plenty of time to consider what to say next. Roni watched as mile after mile of farmland passed before her. Her mother had loved living in Kansas because she could see for miles in all directions. She would say, "Look and see where the earth meets the sky, with nothing in the way. That's what heaven will be like." It would be hard to find another place like that.

"Roni, I know I can't ever make up for... for what I have done in the past. Jason is gone and I can't change that. You are going to have to search your heart to find some forgiveness for me before it eats you up.

"I swear to you, though, that I am not making the stuff up about Michael. He is real. He is the leader of some other angels who are trying to stop Ezekiel and his boss. They have some kind of genetic and robotic human research going on that is changing the human race from the Creator's original design. Michael has defeated them before, so we have a good chance of doing it again. Roni, are you listening to me?"

"Wow. I think you might actually believe this line of boloney you're trying to feed me," she exclaimed. "I am not stupid! Pull this car over and let me out. You are crazy!"

"Roni, wait," began Ryan.

But Roni was feeling for her seatbelt buckle and the door handle.

"No, wait, Roni! There's an exit right up ahead, where we can stop and talk."

Roni quit wriggling around and sat still. Ryan got off at the next exit and pulled into a Wendy's parking lot. The moment he stopped, Roni jumped out of the car and began to run toward the field next to the restaurant.

"Roni, don't run! Your heart can't take it!"

Ryan was running after her, but all Roni could hear was the cold wind blowing in her ears. Tears were pouring down her face. Though her legs felt wobbly, an unexpected burst of energy propelled her farther and farther away from Ryan. She lost track of how long and how far she ran. Western Kansas land is flat for miles in all directions, and it wasn't long before she was lost and feeling totally drained of all energy. But she kept on running. Her legs were burning and her heart felt as if it would leap right out of her chest. She was so confused.

"Why was Ryan making up such a wild story? Are my sisters safe? Who do I trust?"

"You know," the voice said to her.

She stopped running.

"I know what?"

"You know who to trust."

"No, I don't know," she argued back.

"Search your heart, Roni. Don't run from your purpose."

Roni felt her heart fluttering as she began to ask, "What's my purpose?" But even as she asked the question, somehow she already knew the answer to it.

The voice spoke softly to her.

"To live."

***

The light was low in the room when Roni awoke. She recognized where she was. It was the master bedroom in her parents' lake house. The blue suede bedspread reminded Roni of all the times she had crawled into bed with her parents when the lightning outside had scared her. Her hand reached for the familiar charm around her neck.

She could hear whispers. A woman was talking with two men in the hallway near the bedroom door. The woman– who was dark-skinned with long black hair plaited into what looked like hundreds of braids—reminded Roni of the nurse from the hospital. In fact, as she listened to the woman speak, Roni was convinced it was Priscilla.

"What is she doing here?" said Roni to herself. "Is she involved in all this craziness?"

It was as though Priscilla had heard her thoughts. She walked over with the two men into the bedroom.

"O baby, you're awake." Priscilla put her arms around Roni and kissed her on the cheek. "How do you feel? You scared me. Again. You should have known better than to run with your new heart thing! Ryan was beside himself when I carried you back across that field. I wasn't sure Gabriel and Ralph were going to be able to console him. It was a good thing he had some of those shots for you."

"Whoa, wait! You carried me?" said Roni, feeling her chest. It was sore at the injection sites.

She only half believed what she was hearing. Priscilla was maybe five feet tall and barely 100lbs. How could she have lifted her?

"I'm stronger than I look," laughed Priscilla. "Don't judge an angel by her superficial covering."

"Oh yeah. The angel thing," thought Roni.

Her two companions were both very tall, with massive shoulders. They were dressed in casual men's clothing; not at all what Roni would expect angels to be wearing. The blond one seemed a little shy and reserved, while the dark-haired one was warm-hearted and friendly.

"Hi, I'm Raphael. My friends call me Ralph. And this is my friend Gabriel." He held out his hand and Roni reluctantly took it. The other man looked warmly at her.

"Gabriel's a little shy. He tends to get over exuberant in his work. He always has to start every assignment with

"Don't be afraid" or the humans freak out. He gets a lot of hassle from the other angels, he's kind of a boy scout." Ralph's smile was sincere and it put Roni at ease.

"Hello, I'm Roni," she said.

"Ya, we know," said Ralph. "Priscilla talks about you all the time."

"So... you're... all... angels?" Roni asked.

She was still having a hard time trying to accept that she was in the same room as angels. *I mean, if all this was for real?* Gabriel—THE Gabriel—was standing in her parents' bedroom talking... well, not talking, but at least standing there.

"Yes we are," said Ralph, answering her thoughts.

"Why are you here?" asked Roni. "I'm still a little confused. No, wait, I'm a lot confused. I can't wrap my mind around all this."

"Well, we are going to let Ryan explain things to you, but please don't try and run off again. You are in great danger. If you continue to try to get away from us, then we can't help you," said Ralph.

"So you aren't forcing me to stay here?"

Gabriel knelt beside her bed. His voice was like a warm day in spring and it made Roni feel safe. "No. You have the free will to reject our help. The Creator does not force his protection or will on anyone."

"Good job, Gab!" whispered Ralph. "Look. No fear and trembling."

Gabriel blushed a little. Then they heard a short knock at the door. It was Ryan.

"Hey guys, do you mind if I talk to Roni for a little while?"

"I will be right by your door, baby," said Priscilla.

"There are several other Watchers around the house. They have placed a shield around this property," said Gabriel. "You should be safe tonight."

"Thank you, Gabriel," said Roni.

He took her hand. She felt warmth and trust flow through her body.

"You are highly favored by the Lord," he said and then stood up and left.

Ryan came into the bedroom and stood by the end of the bed. "You thoroughly freaked out yet?" he asked.

"Pretty much," she answered. She sat up and Ryan walked over to her and put an extra pillow behind her back. "What is going on, Ryan? Why am I in danger?"

Ryan sat down in the rocking chair by the bed. "You remember I told you about the nanites in your body?"

Roni nodded. "How could I forget?"

"Well, there is more. That spot on your back, I think it's some kind of kill switch."

"Kill switch?" gasped Roni. "To kill what? Me?"

"To put it bluntly, yes," said Ryan.

Roni started to panic again.

"Roni, calm down," Ryan pleaded. "We don't need you getting all worked up again. I don't know all the information on what the kill switch does. I haven't been able to translate all the research documents. Your sisters will be here tomorrow with the rest of the boxes from Norilsk. I have a suspicion that Jeni will be able to assist me in the further translation of the papers."

"So why is all this happening to us?"

"I'm going to tell you what Michael told me. Please just try to have an open mind and not freak out every other sentence, or this will take all night."

"Ok. I will try. But no guarantees."

CHAPTER 8

Under His Wings

*"He will cover you with his feathers, and under
his wings you will find refuge."*

Psalm 91:4a, NIV

"It all started in the Book of Genesis."

"In the Bible?" asked Roni.

"Yes. In Genesis Chapter 6 it says that a group of angels called Watchers, who were supposed to be helping humans, got it into their heads that they wanted to come down to earth and take human wives for themselves because the women were so beautiful. Well, that was against the Creator's design.

"The children that these angels and women had were giants. They were evil, and there wasn't enough food to keep up with their appetites. So they began to cannibalize humans and, when that wasn't enough, they ate each other.

"The angels taught mankind the secrets of the universe that they were not supposed to know. Things were just getting out of hand, and the Creator knew something had to be done. First, he dealt with the angels who had started the problems.

"Michael and some other angels captured most of those rogue Watchers and put them in a sort of holding place until judgment. The children of the angels pretty much wiped each other out, but the Creator wanted all traces of the angelic blood destroyed; so that's where the Great Flood comes in. It was supposed to wipe all that out.

"However, in the Book of Numbers, we find that there were giants among the descendants of Ham in the land again. Also, in 1 Samuel, who could forget the famous story of David and the giant Goliath? Someone started messing with human DNA again. Not as blatantly as before, but there are still traces of angelic or giant DNA in some humans today."

"What about the artificial intelligence robotics thing?" asked Roni. "Is that what's wrong with me? Am I a robot or something that God wants to wipe off the face of the Earth?" She was beginning to get upset again.

"No, you are not a robot but you definitely have had some artificial intelligence put in you. How much or by whom I don't know. Like I said, I need to finish translating the research to find out more."

Roni had a worried expression on her face. He could tell that she was rolling things around in her mind.

"You need to sleep," said Ryan. "Your sisters will be here tomorrow. I'll try not to steal Jeni for too long." He smiled at Roni and left the room.

"What in the world is happening? Everything is upside down," Roni cried out in fear and confusion.

She got out of bed and walked over to the doors that opened onto a little balcony outside. She went over to the ledge and leaned on the railing. Her bare feet were cold on the wooden planks. Looking up at the sky, she could see millions of stars. She put her hand around her necklace charm.

"How can the Creator of the universe make such glorious lights in the sky and still find time to care about me? Am I even his child with these things in me?" she cried out.

A voice behind her spoke. "You are more beautiful to him than all the stars he made for you to enjoy. You are his precious daughter."

Roni turned around and, to her amazement, she saw an enormous angel standing on the ground beside the balcony. His waist was right at the level of the balcony platform. His head towered above her. His gaze was in the direction of the horizon and it never wavered. In his hand, a huge sword was drawn, and he held it as if ready for a fight at any moment. His six magnificent wings were covering part of the house and, as Roni stepped back a little further, she could see a host of angels just as tall and massive as the one next to her. All their wings were connected, forming a translucent, airtight seal around her house.

Out a little farther was another row of these angels, all standing and with their wings spread open, ready to fight. Not only were they protecting the house from a horizontal attack but, as Roni looked up, she could see the backs of hundreds of angel wings, protecting the house from an aerial assault. A verse her mom would say, when the storm outside scared her, came to her mind:

> "He will cover you with his feathers, and under his wings you will find refuge."
>
> *Psalm 91:4a, NIV*

Never again would she have to imagine what that verse meant.

CHAPTER 9

Angels in the House

*"Are not all angels ministering spirits sent to serve
those who will inherit salvation?"*

Hebrews 1:14, NIV

Monday 4ᵗʰ November

Roni slept peacefully all night. She didn't even stir when Ryan came in to check on her around 3am. He listened to her heartbeat for a while. It sounded good. He prayed that he had gotten the pacemaker and serum right. Open heart surgery wasn't a very viable option out in the middle of nowhere.

What was he going to do about this girl? This young woman. He loved her but he couldn't see any way into her heart. All the "if onlys" crowded his already full mind. *If only I had been nicer to her and Jason. If only I hadn't teased them so much. If only I hadn't left Roni alone with Jason's body that night.* Round and round, those regrets would go in his brain till it hurt.

"There are no do-overs," she had said. How could he possibly ask Roni to love him?

He looked at Priscilla as he walked over to the door. She had not left Roni alone since carrying the girl back across the field the previous day. She took him by the hand.

"The Creator has given us charge over her. She is safe," she assured him.

He left the room, closing the door behind him. As he walked down the stairs, he looked at all the family pictures hanging on the walls. Those were happy times for Roni and her sisters. Times that were only memories for them now. Losing a parent had to be the hardest thing a child could go through, and they had lost both within mere months of each other. He still had his parents. True, he had lost Jason at twelve, but that was more of a punishment for him. His baby brother had been so frail all his life, and he had tormented him until the day he died. Ryan wiped a tear from his eye.

He reached the ground floor and saw Gabriel in the family room, keeping watch by the sliding glass doors. Ralph was looking out of the kitchen window. They were as statues guarding a palace. Every room in the house had an angel standing guard. Ryan sat down on the couch.

"What have I walked into?" Ryan said to himself. "What is so important that we have to be guarded by a... a lot of angels? What more am I going to have to tell Roni about the crazy stuff in her body? Help me, Lord. I want to save her so badly."

"He is listening."

It was Gabriel speaking. He came and sat next to Ryan. Ryan was a pretty big guy himself, but he felt like a child next to the immense angel.

"You must trust Him to do the best thing for you and Roni. The Creator loves all his children and will forgive them of their past sins when they ask him to." The angel put his hand on Ryan's shoulder, then said gently, "You must leave Roni in his hands. She will have to stand on her own before this battle is won."

"What is that supposed to mean?" asked Ryan. "Why does she have to stand on her own? Why can't I help her?"

"Each of you must work out your own salvation," said Gabriel. "She has to find her own faith in the Creator. You cannot save Roni's soul, just as she cannot save yours. We all come to the Creator in our own special way. He has designed each of us uniquely for his own purpose. You will only be fulfilled physically and spiritually when you are doing the thing you were created for."

"You are right, of course. Never argue with a seven-foot angel," said Ryan, laughing a little. "You're getting this human relation thing down, Gabe."

Gabriel smiled and stood up to take his post again. Ryan lay down on the couch to get some rest. He slept a little easier after his talk with Gabriel.

Gabriel looked toward the heavens. "Lord of Hosts," he prayed. "Please protect these children of yours in doing the task you have laid before them. Make your Watchers strong, that we may protect them and glorify your wondrous name. Amen."

***

Roni awoke early the next morning, just before the sun rose. She walked over to the balcony doors. She wondered if the angel would still be there. He was, and so were the rest of the Watchers.

Down in the kitchen, Roni could see that someone had done their homework on human cuisine.

"Plenty of Yoo-hoo and pizza hot pockets, food fit for a king," she giggled aloud as she took a large sip of Yoo-hoo.

Shutting the door of the refrigerator, she suddenly saw Ralph standing right in front of her. Roni was so startled she spilt Yoo-hoo all over him.

"Oh, oh my! I'm so sorry! I didn't even see you there. You can't sneak up on people like that." She grabbed a roll of paper towels and tried to clean up the angel's shirt. "Oh gosh, I hope I don't get... like... some kind of... angelic penalty for this!"

Gabriel snickered from the other room. "Who's frightening the humans now, Ralph?"

"Interesting," Roni said. "Angelic humor. I never thought I'd see that."

"You should have seen the pranks we played on Michael back in the Garden of Eden days. They were epic!" exclaimed Ralph. He and Gabriel looked at each other like two mischievous schoolboys.

"Remember the time we got the Pegasus to fly over with the honey?"

They were both laughing so hard now that Roni joined in.

"He was picking honey out of his wings for a week!"

"Ah, yes. Back in the days before Lucifer messed everything up (now, that's an example of how a little jealousy can go a LONG way). There was no sin then, and the entire world was in harmony with the Creator."

The angels looked sad for a moment; then Gabriel said, "I'm looking forward to those days again."

"Me too," said Ralph.

"Has anyone seen Prisc..." Roni started to say as she turned around.

"Right here, baby, never left your side."

Priscilla was definitely a morning person.

"Wow... ok..." said Roni. "Humans are a little funny when it comes to personal space. You don't have to be quite so close. I promise I won't run away without you."

"You'd better not, sweetheart," she kissed Roni on the cheek.

"Ralph, do you know when my sisters will be here?"

"Well, Michael and Uriel were supposed to get them all packed up last night, so I think they should get here sometime later this morning."

"What?! Michael took Uriel? He's going to frighten those babies to death," exclaimed Priscilla.

"Especially if he hasn't put those flaming swords away," said Gabriel. "You guys think I'm scary; wait till you see Uriel. He stood at the Gate of Eden, with those flaming swords of his, for weeks after Adam and Eve got thrown out. He took that whole incident very hard."

Ryan heard the angels and Roni laughing heartily. It was good to hear her laugh again. When he entered the kitchen, her eyes met his and she became quiet. She wasn't sure what to do; so she just gave him a little smile and then looked away.

"Well, we'd better get some breakfast going, so I can get the girls' rooms ready before they get here," she said. "What does everyone want?"

"You don't have to feed us," said Ralph. "It isn't necessary for us to consume food." He looked down at the floor.

"Oh stop," said Priscilla. "You know you want to eat. The Creator hasn't forbidden us to eat with humans. He himself ate with Abraham. How about some bacon, eggs and grits? Gabe? Ralph? Ryan?"

They all nodded back in unison.

"All right, baby, let's get this going."

The three angels and two humans gave thanks to the Creator and had an enjoyable breakfast. Afterwards, Ryan went to set up a workroom in the basement for his research, and the angels went to check on the security of the property. Priscilla and Roni stayed to clean up the kitchen.

"How long have you been my guardian angel?" asked Roni shyly. She wasn't sure how to pose that question.

"Well, back when you had just come to life. In your mother's womb," answered Priscilla.

"You knew my birth mother?" asked Roni excitedly.

Priscilla stopped working and looked at Roni with tears in her eyes. "Yes, dear," she replied, as tears began to flow down her face. "I was her angel before I was yours. She died giving birth to you. She was so young, only fourteen. I pleaded with the Creator to let her live, but He knew she had had a hard life."

"She had suffered so much, and she was ready to go to her reward. She loved and worshipped the Creator all of her life, and then," Priscilla smiled, "I got to take her to those pearly gates, as you humans say. She was so happy to be with the only Father she had ever known, the Creator. I'll never forget looking back one last time before I came back to be with you. I saw her sitting on his lap and they were singing together. Her eyes sparkled. Her beautiful hair was blowing in the breeze. No more pain. No more crying."

Roni looked at the angel. A glow was on her face as she spoke of heaven and the Creator.

"You are a lot like her. Brown hair and eyes. Same determination and sweetness of spirit. I can't wait till you meet her."

Roni had never thought about that. "I will see her someday. My mother and father too. And Jason!" The thought of that made her smile.

"Come with me. There is someone I want you to meet," said Priscilla, leading her back upstairs and out onto the balcony. "I want you to meet Oriel. He was Jason's guardian angel."

CHAPTER 10

Guardian Angels

"Herein is love, not that we loved God, but that he loved us, and sent his Son to be the propitiation for our sins."

1 John 4:10

Roni wasn't sure what to say. Jason had been gone six years. She had never forgotten that last night in the woods with Ryan and Jason. One minute they were playing and the next Jason was lying on the ground. There wasn't even a goodbye. He was dead before he hit the ground. Then it started raining and she was alone with him until morning. She had never forgiven Ryan for leaving her. Her mind was racing, but her thoughts were interrupted by the approach of a huge angel.

Priscilla introduced him as Oriel.

"I am so honored to meet you. Jason spoke so highly of you," Oriel said.

"He did? I didn't know you guys had talked. He never mentioned it," said Roni.

"Some things you were not ready to hear. Jason knew that. He loved you so much."

Roni started crying. Priscilla held her close. Then Oriel put his arms around her and comforted her.

"Jason knew his time on this earth was short," said Oriel. "Only twelve years to fulfill his purpose."

"His purpose?" said Roni sharply, and she pushed herself away from the angel. "He was only twelve years old. He barely lived, and the time he was here he was so sick he couldn't do anything, let alone fulfill a purpose!" she cried, exposing the bitterness and anger she had been nurturing in her soul.

"Roni," said Priscilla, "your love for Jason has clouded your spiritual sight. You can't stop seeing the weak little boy. Let Oriel minister to your soul. He knew Jason as well as you. And he loved him as much."

Roni stood with her back to Priscilla and Oriel for a while. Angels are not short on patience. They waited for her. She wasn't sure what to say, now that she had behaved in such a discourteous way. After a few minutes, she turned around with her head hung down.

"I'm sorry. I shouldn't have said that. Tell me about the Jason you knew."

They sat for about half an hour, telling Jason stories. They laughed and they cried. Finally Roni mustered up the courage to ask Oriel a question she had never even considered before.

"What was Jason's purpose?" asked Roni.

Oriel paused a moment. A tear slid down his enormous cheek. Then he smiled and looked deeply into her dark brown eyes. "To love you," he said.

There was silence as Roni pondered over the angel's statement.

"Unconditionally," he added. "So that one day you could understand the Creator's unconditional love. A love uninhibited by anything you could ever do or say."

Roni thought about the meaning of uninhibited love. "How is that possible?" she asked. "There always seems to be something in the way when it comes to loving people."

"When you have learnt to love someone, uninhibited by their past mistakes, then you will have understood the love the Creator has for his children. All his children," Uriel added, "including the liars, thieves, murderers and child abusers."

"I think the children are here," Priscilla interrupted.

"Maybe we could talk again sometime," said Roni to Oriel, "about Jason. Or other stuff too." She hugged the massive angel once more and he smiled at her.

***

"Roni... Roni... Roni!" The three girls ran to embrace their sister.

"It's been a hundred years since we saw you!" exclaimed Zoei.

"It does seem like forever," said Juli.

"I've missed you all so much!" exclaimed Roni.

The girls hugged each other tightly for about five minutes.

"Ok babies, let's get you inside," said Priscilla.

"She likes to mother," whispered Roni to her sisters. "It's kind of nice."

Once everyone was indoors, it was obvious that introductions needed to be made. If the family room were any smaller, the meeting would have had to be outside. Seven-foot angels are not so easy to seat in a house meant for five- to six-foot humans.

Gabriel spoke first in a tone of great respect. "Michael, this is the human, Roni. Roni, this is Michael the Archangel."

Roni was definitely in awe of this enormous creature who commanded respect just by standing in the room. His eyes were blue and his hair was black as night.

"And his companion is Uriel."

The second angel was also very remarkable. Tall and dark-skinned, compared to the other angels. Roni looked for the famous flaming swords.

"I am pleased to make the acquaintance of one so favored by our Creator," Michael said. "I've only seen you from a distance, so I am happy to finally meet you."

61

All were silent. They hardly dared to breathe, let alone speak. Roni leaned over to Priscilla and whispered, "I feel like I should be on my knees or something."

"No," Priscilla answered. "It is not for you to worship us. Only the Creator is worthy of such an honor. Michael has fought and won many battles and is definitely worthy of respect, but NEVER is an angel to be worshipped."

"I'm... um... really pleased and glad to meet both of you," said Roni nervously.

"The pleasure is ours," Uriel answered. He felt a tug on his pants and looked down. It was Zoei.

"Mr U-ie, I need another piggyback ride," the child looked up at him with such innocence the angel could not refuse.

"Be prepared to work in an hour," said Michael to the other angels. "The children's protectors will remain with them AT ALL TIMES. You are dismissed."

"Mr U-ie?" Ralph whispered to Gabriel. Both covered their mouths and laughed as they poked fun at the other angel. Uriel flashed his dark eyes at them. The message for them to quit was loud and clear.

Priscilla introduced the other guardians to Roni. "This is Samuel, Jeni's guardian; Ariel, Juli's guardian; and Priel, Zoei's guardian."

Samuel and Priel looked like strong farm boys. They had a sense of duty and honor about them that made Roni feel at ease. Jeni and Zoei would be well cared for. Juli's protector, on the other hand, was a small-framed girl with long, flowing blond hair, and Roni swore she heard music every time she talked.

"Remember, don't judge an angel by her superficial coverings," said Priscilla. "Ariel can be a fierce opponent in battle. She wields the battle axe like you can't believe."

"Battle axe? Sweet!" said Roni to Ariel, who smiled back shyly.

***

Michael and Uriel had done a great job of getting the stuff that Roni and her sisters were going to need. They had even packed the girls' Bibles.

"Do they think we can go to church out here?" Roni laughed as she put the Bibles aside.

"Clothes, clothes, clothes, is that all girls think about?" said Samuel to Priel.

"And shoes!" said Priel. "How many girls are staying here? Only four? You could outfit over half the angels in heaven with what I just put away."

"I don't know how they can get anything else done," Samuel said. "Now I know why Oriel always goes for the male guardian assignments."

"Watch it, boys," said Ariel. "The softer side of creation knows how to be fierce and look good doing it."

Juli leaned over to Jeni and said, "My guardian is so cool!"

The girls all laughed. They spent the next hour putting away clothes and making beds for the three sisters to sleep in. Juli had bathroom duty. It had been so long since any of them had been to the lake house that the bathroom drawers had to be divided up again. It was Zoei's first time at the house, so there was plenty for an inquisitive five-year-old to explore.

Since Roni was the oldest, she had the privilege of staying in her parents' bedroom. Her younger sisters were glad to let her have it, considering how much she had given up for them over the last year.

"Thanks, guys, for all your help. The rooms look great," said Jeni.

Then, turning to Priel, she asked, ""This might be a silly question, but do angels sleep?"

"Not in the same sense that humans do," replied Priel. "We know how to conserve our energy, and we discipline ourselves to rest and reserve our strength until it is needed."

"Kinda like firemen," said Jeni. "Most of the time when we went to the firehouse in the afternoon we had to be quiet because, if the men were there, they were napping."

"Good observation," Priel said.

"Why anyone would want to sleep on purpose on a perfectly fabulous day such as this is beyond me," Zoei interjected.

Everyone was quiet for a few seconds, then a big shout of laughter was heard throughout the house. The angels looked at each other and it seemed they were strengthened by the exuberance of the humans.

"Laughter is a natural medicine given by the Creator. Human laughter gives pleasure to a guardian's heart," said Ariel.

"Like music," said Roni, and she looked at Juli and Ariel.

"Exactly," they said at the same time.

A red-headed angel stuck his head around the door. "Michael would like to see you now, Roni," he said.

Roni got quiet and swallowed hard. She was suddenly very nervous.

"It's ok, baby. Michael would never harm you. Just be calm and speak truthfully to him. You are more important than you know." Priscilla stroked Roni's hair as she spoke.

Roni stood up and began her descent downstairs.

"Michael the Archangel," she thought to herself. "I wonder if he can read my mind. Can he 'smite' people down? What if I make him mad?"

"That's unlikely," said the angel in front of her.

"I didn't say anything," said Roni.

"You don't have to. We can hear your thoughts."

Roni stopped cold by the basement door.

"What?" she tried to turn around and run, but Priscilla was in her way.

"Wait, Roni. Remember, no running."

"But Michael can..."

"Yes, I know," said Priscilla. "It would take us an eternity if we had to wait for you to say what you are really thinking, and half the time you wouldn't or couldn't be honest. Just relax. I'll be there every step of the way."

They continued downstairs. When they got there, Roni had a hard time believing they were in her basement. There were papers hung up everywhere. Drawings of people, like in a science class, telling what was beneath the skin. Diagrams of small machines and formulas for what looked like medicine as well. Then there was writing, page after page, in some foreign language.

"Jeni will make short work of this, I bet," she said to herself.

"Roni, please come join us," Michael welcomed her.

She walked over to where Michael the Archangel was seated together with Ryan.

"Be at peace, child. There is no reason to fear. Please sit down."

Sitting down at a small table in the corner with Ryan and Michael was a little intimidating, but the angel's caring ways soon set her at ease.

"I know Ryan has told you how we met and why we are together," the Archangel began. "The battle for the soul of mankind has been ongoing almost since the Creator said the first 'Let there be'.

"The Dark One took a third of the angels with him that dreadful day in Eden. Another two hundred were locked away by me a short time before the Flood. These Watchers had broken the Creator's law and taken human women for wives. The result was the creation of a sort of superhuman race, the Nephilim. They were evil and the land could not sustain them. They consumed the humans and each other, but their appetites could not be satisfied. The offspring that did survive were killed off in the Great Flood.

"The Creator's own heart was so crushed with what had taken place that he swore an oath never again to destroy the Earth by water. And he has kept that promise. He has even put safeguards in place so that humans won't be able to commit the same abominations as before the Flood. One is shortened life spans. With shortened lives, no human will be able to process a problem for five hundred years and come up with a solution.

"Second," continued Michael, "was putting the fear of humans in animals and vice versa. When humans and animals started to fear each other, it took people more time and effort to obtain subjects for their experiments. The Creator also confounded their languages, and that scattered them over the face of the whole Earth. Sometime later the children of Ham, who had been cursed by Noah, attempted the rebirth of giants again.

"The threat of a worldwide infiltration has not been seen in centuries. Every now and then, evil dictators rise up; but they are struck down by humans who defend the weak. The Dark One's desire to create a super race has cost some groups of humans dearly. The Jews were nearly erased from the face of the earth in the first half of the twentieth century. The slaughter of Christians began almost immediately following the birth of the church, but it has never been fully realized by the people of this country. Millions of believers have been killed worldwide for the cause of the Creator and his Son.

The angel paused for a moment and looked at them as though he was staring into their souls.

"I want to tell you two that you are both at risk of losing your own hearts and souls," he stated gravely, stopping for a few moments to let the reality of what he had just said sink in.

Ryan stood up suddenly. "What? I have not given myself over to any of these evil angels or people!" he shouted defensively. The whole room grew quiet.

"Please give us the room," said Michael, and instantly all the other angels vanished. The archangel stood up and went over to Ryan. He put his hands on the young man's shoulders.

"Ryan, the Dark One wants to take you to the edge of your humanity, just to see if you will jump off. He will toy with you and use your loved ones against you. This is why I am here, to warn you and to equip you to do battle with his evil forces. You and Roni's involvement was decided for you long ago. Now it is up to the two of you to choose who will control your future. Will it be you and your selfish human desires or will you allow the Creator to guide your destinies? Will you let him give you beauty in the place of the ashes the Dark One has thrown over your lives?

"You have power, Ryan. Power you do not even begin to understand. In the operating room, when you held

Roni's heart in your hands, *you* caused her heart to beat again. Not the Creator. Because of the selective breeding done in your bloodline, you can heal people of sicknesses and injuries."

Michael looked next at Roni. "Juli can sing and understand music. Jeni can read and understand languages. It is part of their genetic design. The traces of angelic blood left in their bodies allow them to do tricks. Tricks that are meant to seduce them. Stroke their egos. Make them think they can do anything on their own without the Creator's help.

"Those supernatural gifts must be surrendered to the Creator, only to be used for his glory; otherwise, those gifts will kill and destroy your sisters and everyone else in their path."

Michael sat down again. He looked back at Roni, who had a look of shock on her face.

"I never... they never..." was all she could say.

"I know," said Michael. "You and your sisters never asked for this."

He paused for a moment and looked deeply into Roni's eyes. "I have no idea what your half-human half-artificial intelligence body can do. Only that..." he broke off abruptly and stood up.

"What is it?" asked Ryan.

"He is here," said Michael.

"Who?" asked Roni.

"Ezekiel."

Michael hit his chest over his heart and said, "The sword of the Lord!" Immediately a huge sword was in his hand.

Then he disappeared.

CHAPTER 11

The Evil Angel

"The angel of the LORD encampeth round about them that fear him, and delivereth them."

Psalm 34:7

Roni and Ryan were up the basement stairs in three seconds, and what they saw when they reached the top left them breathless.

Everyone was outside. About a hundred yards away stood Uriel, a flaming sword in each hand. He had shed his earthly appearance, yet the humans still recognized him. His flesh appeared as molten gold and he stood at least fifteen feet tall. He had on a breastplate and body armor made of some silvery metal. A white, loose-fitting sort of kilt hung around his waist, almost to his knees. His silver helmet was gleaming, with dark red tassels adorning its top. Under his feet sat the small form of a girl being cared for by a much less terrifying angel. Priel.

"ZOEI!" screamed Roni.

Ryan held her back with all his strength. She tore at him wildly to get loose, for she saw the creature that stood before Uriel. Another angel of equal might, with a dagger in one hand and a sword in the other. A crimson dragon was on his breastplate and his kilt was black as coal. At once Roni knew it was Ezekiel.

"I will leave the child alone, but I want something in return. The girl, the one I left my mark on," Ezekiel bartered, his speech sly and smooth.

Roni's face began to burn. The white star-like spot on her cheek started to pulse and burn brightly. She clutched her face and fell to the ground, crying out in agony from the pain. Priscilla tried to comfort her.

"You shall have neither the girl nor her sister," said Uriel to his opponent. "You have not been away so long as to forget the last time we crossed swords. I recognize H'imesh-Dagon from the knick I left in him the last time we battled."

"You were lucky then," hissed Ezekiel as he looked at the blade of his sword. A small gouge near the hilt was darkened around its edges and dulled, compared to the rest of the weapon. "Now you hide behind the skirts of a human child."

"I am not hiding. I will not cower behind anyone or anything to protect the children of the Creator," replied Uriel. His voice was steady but powerful as the other angel tried to provoke him.

Suddenly Ezekiel rose up in the air, his three pairs of white wings shining bright in the Kansas afternoon sky. "I will end the life of this child and take her sister. She was meant to be mine! And I will defeat you once and for all!"

As Ezekiel lifted his weapons in the air, Uriel assumed an "at ready" stance. He spoke to his flaming swords: "Make your mark swift and true, A'met. Bring honor to the Creator, K'vod."

Roni surveyed the scene and felt the panic rise in her. She made no sound but got up and, without a word, began to run with all her might toward Zoei. Her speed was almost superhuman. From behind her, she felt the ground shake.

"In the name of the Lord!" Michael shouted.

He shed his human appearance and joined her in the frontal assault. His armor, like Uriel's, glinted in the sunlight. The crimson lion on their breastplates set them apart from Ezekiel's dragon.

Roni hit her chest and cried out, "The sword of the Lord!"

Nothing happened. Her hand reached out in front of her and, as if by sheer will power, a blue ball of light appeared in the palm of her hand.

Ten feet before he reached Uriel, Michael jumped, and the swords of all three angels connected in one sonic boom. The downward blast of sound slammed Roni to the ground, but she had managed to release the ball of light before she was immobilized. It exploded in a burst of shimmering blue confetti that landed on everything.

"Ha, ha, ha! I knew she could do it!" shouted Ezekiel. He was being held back, about fifty feet in the air, by Michael and Uriel. "We did it! The souls of men are doomed! Come, my daughter, we will dominate heaven and earth!"

Roni looked up. Her ears were bleeding and she could not hear anything. She saw Ezekiel holding out his hand to her. *No!* She shook her head and backed away from the enormous creature.

"You are mine! I created you!" shouted Ezekiel. "Nothing can keep us apart!"

He backed away from Michael and Uriel. "And you two can't stop it," he roared. With this parting shot, the evil angel leapt up and out of the atmosphere.

Roni tried to stand up, but she just wobbled and fell back over. Her eyes could not seem to focus on anything anymore. Finally she gave up and lay on her back, staring up at the blue sky. Someone's face was hovering over her, but she couldn't remember who it was. The woman seemed familiar, but she couldn't quite place her. Then a young man was staring down at her. He seemed to be talking, but she couldn't hear any sounds at all.

The lady helped her to sit up. The man put his hands over both of her ears. He was still talking, but not to her, to someone above her. She looked but saw no one. Then her ears began to feel hot. She tried to back away from the man, but the woman held her in place. A buzzing sound started getting louder and louder in her ears. Then... Pop!

Roni jumped up.

"It's ok, Roni. You're ok," said Ryan.

She continued to stagger as she tried to regain her balance.

"What happened?" she yelled, as her hearing hadn't completely healed yet.

"You're ok, baby," said Priscilla reassuringly. "Everyone is safe."

"What happened?" she yelled again.

"You are an insane idiot is what happened!" yelled Ryan, and he grabbed her arms to steady her.

"What were you thinking, running out on the middle of a fight between twenty-foot angels with flaming swords and knives? And what was with the blue ball of light thing? You could have killed us all."

"Her bravery is commendable; however, it was foolish to go into battle ill-equipped," said Michael. He was back in his more humanlike form. "You must learn to control your instincts when it comes to your abilities. We will talk later. She needs rest. Priscilla, please tend to your charge."

"Yes sir. Child, you are going to be the death of me!" the guardian exclaimed. "I thought we agreed that you weren't going to run away again?"

"I wasn't technically running away," said Roni. "I was running *to* Zoei. Nobody else was going after her," she muttered the last sentence, glaring at Ryan.

"What?" he said irately. "You expected me to run out in the middle of an angel swordfight? That sounds like a brilliant plan. I run out there and get squashed like a bug and Zoei still ends up dead. What good would any of that have done?"

Roni was toe to toe with him once more. "It might show some people that you cared about others more than yourself. But then we know how you feel about dead bodies, don't we?"

Those last words cut Ryan like a knife.

"You're never going to let me forget that, are you? I keep asking myself: what I can do to get you to forgive me? What can I do to make up for that night?"

"Seven hours," she said slowly and backed away from him. "Seven hours you left me there. Seven hours, in the rain, with Jason's dead body. You want to know what you can do to make up for that? NOTHING!" she screamed.

"Nothing can erase that night. Nothing!" She turned and ran away.

Ryan just stood there. He wasn't sure what to do. All hope of love with Roni seemed gone. He would never hold her as his own. She hated him. He couldn't even prove to her that he was a man now. He hadn't even tried to save Zoei. "Maybe I am a coward," thought Ryan.

He turned to walk away but Oriel was standing in his way. "I guess you heard all that?" Ryan said.

"Hmm," said Oriel. "Sounded like a pity party to me."

"What do you know about it?" shouted Ryan. "What do angels know of human heartbreak? You don't get married, have families, no brothers or sisters to worry about. Do you even love?"

Ryan was taunting Oriel and trying to provoke him. But he could not.

"You are mistaken if you think angels do not love. We love. We hate. We are happy and we are sad. We cry, laugh, suffer and rejoice. We are tempted to break the Creator's laws when it would please us."

"Then why does it seem like you guys have it all together?" Ryan sat on a bench on the back patio with his head in his hands.

"We discipline our minds and actions," said Oriel as he sat next to Ryan. "It is not always easy. Sometimes it takes great pain to go against our own will in order to do the will of the Creator; but we do it, day by day, a little at a time."

"I'm a cardiac surgeon and I can't even care for the heart of the girl I love," said Ryan. "Painful irony, huh?"

"One thing I know about the Creator is that, not only is he wise above all his creation, he has a great sense of irony too. For a hundred years, Abraham had no children; but his name meant 'father of many'. It took a Hebrew prisoner to save the world from famine. A prince with a stutter to free a nation from slavery. And a child born in a manger to become King of the Universe."

Ryan looked at Oriel. "Can you teach me to be wise, to be disciplined... to be a man?"

"Yes, I can. But you must first surrender your life to the Creator," said Oriel.

"How do I begin?" asked Ryan.

"With your mouth. Confess with your mouth that the Creator is your Master and that you give him control of your life."

"That doesn't sound too hard."

"Saying it is the easy part. Doing it will be the hardest task you will ever take on."

"Is there anything else?" asked Ryan.

Oriel laughed out loud. "Yes my child, much more. But let us start here. Do you have your sword?"

"Ahh, I don't own a sword. I'm not really a Lord of the Rings type of guy," said Ryan.

"I'm sorry. You humans call it a Bible. Do you have one?"

"My mom sent me one on my fourteenth birthday. I don't even know where it is," confessed Ryan.

"Don't worry, I saw one in the house. I think it belonged to Roni's dad. Maybe she will let you use it," said Oriel.

"Oh great, that means I have to talk to her," he moaned. "I think I'm on her hate list right now."

"I am sure she will let you use it if you ask later. Just give her a chance to cool down. I think Priscilla is talking to her now," Oriel smiled. "I would much rather have a human male to protect than a female, all those hormones."

Ryan laughed. Then he got serious.

"Oriel, are you my Protector?

"Of course I am."

CHAPTER 12

Pride—and Forgiveness

*"For if ye forgive men their trespasses, your
heavenly Father will also forgive you: But if ye
forgive not men their trespasses, neither will
your Father forgive your trespasses."*

Matthew 6:14-15

The hot shower did Roni good. The dirt had been smashed into her skin. She literally had to scrub it off. She washed her hair three times before the water ran clear. All the blood had been cleaned out of her ears. She had what felt like a burn on the palm of her right hand. Adrenaline was still flowing through her body but its effects had slowly begun to lessen.

"What were you thinking, Roni?" she said to herself. "Running out there onto that field? You could have been killed. Then what would become of your sisters?" She started to cry.

"Why me? Why my family? I'm too young to be responsible for the lives of three other children. I'm practically still a child myself. My classmates have already graduated. They are off at college living their lives, driving around in their fancy trucks, wearing designer clothes. The only decision they have to make is what restaurant they are going to eat at."

"You sound like you are feeling sorry for yourself." It was that voice in her head again.

"Who are you and why are you in my head?" asked Roni.

"Search your heart. You know who I am," said the voice. "Do you really desire such an ordinary life? Eating, driving and shopping?"

76

"Some days that sounds like such an easy life," cried Roni, "just to be a regular teenager, with a mom and dad to take care of me and my sisters."

"I know, my darling. The life I have in mind for you is hard but full of great rewards. I want to do marvelous things through you. I want you to have an extraordinary life. Just trust in me. I will never leave you."

Suddenly a bang on the door broke Roni's concentration.

"You are using all the hot water, Roni. Other people want to get cleaned up too." It was Jeni.

"Oh sorry!" said Roni. "I lost track of time. Be out in a minute." She jumped out of the shower and grabbed her robe, which was hanging on the towel rack.

Roni opened the bathroom door. "I'm really sorry," she apologized.

Jeni, Juli and Zoei were standing right outside the door when it opened.

"Roni Susan Chambers! Don't you ever do that again!" cried Juli.

"What? I said I'm sorry. There's still some hot water left!" She was confused. Juli never got angry, let alone yelled at anyone.

"She means, don't you ever go chasing after bad angels by yourself again without telling anyone!" cried Jeni. "Especially when there are a hundred good angels standing around that can pulverize him in a second!"

"You can't die, Roni," said Zoei, and she reached over to her sister from Jeni's arms. She laid her head on Roni's shoulder. The girls stood there for a while, just holding each other. The loss of one of them would hurt the others so deeply, the pain could not be imagined.

"I won't do that again. I promise," said Roni. "You girls stay close to the house, though. Don't go wandering off into the woods."

"I'm sorry, Roni," said Zoei. "I was chasing a fabulous bunny rabbit. Priel tried to get me to stay by the house but I... I... couldn't resist the power of the bunny!"

Roni smiled at her baby sister and kissed her on the head. "Well, next time, you listen to Priel and ask one of us to go with you too, ok?"

"Ok," answered Zoei. "What about Mr U-ie? Can he take me?"

The older sisters couldn't help but laugh at the thought of Uriel chasing "fabulous" bunny rabbits around.

"Of course that's ok," Roni replied. "Now you three go get cleaned up."

"Thanks, Roni," Zoei said. "You are almost as fabulous as Mr U-ie!"

The girls went to take their baths. As Roni dressed, she thought of thanking Michael, Uriel and Priel for saving Zoei's life—and hers as well.

"Let me look at your hand," Priscilla said to Roni. Roni obediently held out her hand to the angel.

"This looks like something Ryan should see to. Let's go to him."

"No," said Roni, and she pulled her hand away. "No. I don't want to see him."

"You are letting your pride get in the way again, baby," said Priscilla in a very motherly tone. "Are you going to let that pride control the rest of your life?"

Roni was silent as she looked away from Priscilla.

"Child, you are as stubborn as Balaam. Do I need to go find a donkey to talk to you?"

Still Roni was silent.

"Ok, baby girl, it's time for Mama Priscilla to talk."

"You are not my mother," said Roni in a hateful voice. "I don't understand why God took my mother away. She was a great person, always kind to others, the best mom ever. All those other bad mothers get to live while my mom dies. Why? Why? Why?"

She buried her face in her hands, sank down to the floor, and cried. Priscilla knelt down beside her and stroked her hair.

"We don't always know why some things happen, but I do know that the Creator works it all out for the good of his children in the end—yes, even the death of your loved ones. Just trust him."

Roni pondered over what Priscilla had said. Somehow, the angel's words had comforted her. Then, to change the subject, she said, "You know Ryan's parents are still alive, and up until a few weeks ago he hadn't seen them in six years? I can never see my parents again and he would barely speak to them when they came to see me in the hospital."

She thought that, if she talked about Ryan, she could deflect Priscilla's attention from herself. The angel was aware of this.

"Ryan and his parents have some settling up to do, but that is none of your concern. However, if you want to discuss Ryan, let's talk about your mean and unforgiving attitude towards him," said Priscilla. Roni was tongue-tied as she knew Priscilla was about to speak the truth.

"He has made a genuine effort to show his sorrow for the way he used to be," Priscilla pressed on. "The guilt over leaving you and Jason has nearly torn his insides in two. He hasn't seen his parents in years because he can't forgive himself for what he was like toward you and Jason.

He has saved your life a hundred times over. He loves you more than his own flesh—and all you have for him is 'there are no do-overs'?

"I would think long and hard, Roni Chambers, before I dismiss anyone as being undeserving of my love and forgiveness. And, don't forget, the way you forgive others is the same way the Creator will forgive you."

Priscilla's words had gone deep down into Roni's soul. The correction was excruciating to hear, but Roni knew it was true. Because Ryan had hurt her so badly, she had decided he wasn't good enough for her forgiveness. She thought herself so much better than him, but it was her own selfishness that had kept him away from his parents.

When she considered how great the loss of her own parents had been to her, she wept to think that she had denied Ryan that earthly comfort. All because she blamed him for something he couldn't control—Jason's death. She felt great remorse as she realized that she had become the dragon in their story.

"You are right, Priscilla," she said softly. "I have thought myself better than Ryan all these years but now I see that, by not forgiving him, I have kept us both in pain and bondage."

She looked at Priscilla and then held on to her tightly. "I don't want to be that way anymore, Priscilla. Help me to do what is right. Show me how to love uninhibitedly."

"Then free Ryan of his guilt, and both of you will be saved from a life of despair."

Roni knew that Priscilla had spoken the truth. She pulled away from her and said, "Can I start right now?"

"You know you can, baby girl," Priscilla assured her joyfully.

"Then let's go see Dr Miller. My hand is killing me."

CHAPTER 13

The Sword of the Lord

*"And he said unto me, My grace is sufficient for thee:
for my strength is made perfect in weakness."*

2 Corinthians 12:9a

Ryan examined her hand, trying hard not to cause her even more pain.

"It looks like a burn," he finally said. "Did you have this before the ball of light in your hand?"

"No," said Roni. "I didn't even notice it until I was in the shower."

"How much does it hurt? Does it feel like a regular burn?"

"It feels like I touched an iron real fast," answered Roni. "Fast, but not fast enough to escape scorching my hand a little bit."

"Well, let me see if I can heal it."

He took her hand gently in his. Roni pulled it back.

"Heal it? Is that ok with Michael? He did say to be careful with our powers."

"You mean, like you were with the ball of light thing?" Ryan laughed.

She was a little embarrassed.

"It's ok. How do you think your eardrums got repaired, silly?" said Ryan. "You wouldn't be walking upright if I hadn't fixed them."

"Ok then, I trust you," Roni said slowly.

She looked straight into his eyes. It took a lot of will power for her to say that to him, but she knew she had to start somewhere in her endeavor to forgive him.

Ryan's heart skipped a beat. He began to stroke her hand lightly. He looked up, closed his eyes, and spoke softly. "Lord God, Creator of the universe, if it is your will, I ask you to take the power that is within me and heal Roni's hand."

Roni looked at this boy, this man facing her, as he presented her case to the Creator of the world. As if she should ever ask or want another thing from him. He had saved her life and now he was pleading her case once again. No, it was her turn to give him something, but what?

"Nothing is happening," said Ryan. "I don't understand. In the field, I called on the Creator and he answered."

"The Creator is answering you, Ryan," said Michael. No one had noticed that he was in the room until he spoke.

"Sometimes the Creator says no. We do not know why, but often, when he says no, he is asking for our faith in Him to grow. Like he told Paul in the Scriptures, 'My grace is sufficient for you.' He will give you the faith to deal with an answer you didn't want."

There was silence in the room as Ryan treated the burn. Both Roni and Ryan pondered what the angel had said. *Doesn't the Creator want us to be well? Why would he withhold healing from his children?*

Neither of them could comprehend what had happened—or rather, what had *not* happened. Their thoughts were interrupted by Michael.

"It is time for you to learn some self-defense. We will go outside. Roni, gather your sisters and meet us there. Do not forget to bring your swords... I mean your Bibles."

"Yes, Michael," she said. "Oh, do you want Zoei too?

"Of course, since she will be doing most of the teaching," he replied cryptically. Then he turned and walked outside, and they were left to wonder...

What could Zoei teach the rest of them about self-defense? Hadn't Ezekiel almost killed her?

***

The sun was shining and there was a soft southwest wind blowing. The ground looked as though two crop circles had been formed out in the field. One was in the place where the angels' swords had crossed and the other was where Roni's blue ball of light had exploded. She looked at her hand and remembered how it had looked like blue birthday confetti falling from the sky.

"Alright, let us begin with a question," said Michael. "Ryan, if you were faced with an opponent much bigger and stronger than you, let us say an angel like Ezekiel, what would you do?"

Ryan squirmed a bit.

"Um... well... I would look for a weak spot in the armor... maybe... try and get a weapon and kill him?"

"You cannot kill an angel," said Michael. "You can temporarily weaken or restrain him, but you cannot kill him. The only way an angel can die is for him to willingly offer up his *essentia*."

"Oh," Ryan said. His curiosity was aroused. "What is an *essentia*?"

"An *essentia*, to put it in human terms, is the soul of an angel. It is our being. Unlike human souls, which are imperishable, our souls can be extinguished. We can willingly offer our *essentia* up for whatever or whomever we deem worthy."

"Has anyone ever done it?" asked Juli, who was also fascinated by this new piece of information.

"A few," responded Michael. His countenance grew somber and his eyes moistened as he looked off into the distance.

Roni recognized the expression of heartache and wondered if the angel was remembering a great pain in his life. Ryan remembered how he had accused Oriel of not understanding human emotions. He felt ashamed as he watched Michael's grief-stricken face. The children were silent as they watched this regal being feeling the weight of sorrow. After a few moments, Michael regained his composure.

"Roni, what about you?"

"Maybe use some of my powers," she started. "To... like... distract him, and then I could... I really don't know."

"Jeni? Juli? What would you do?"

The twins looked at each other and nodded. They turned back to Michael and said in unison, "RUN!"

Michael laughed. "Great minds think alike, huh? Zoei, tell us what you did today when Mr Ezekiel tried to get to you?"

"I remembered what my mama taught me from the Bible. If I'm afraid, call out to the Creator and He would help me," Zoei replied.

"And did you do that?" Michael asked.

"Yes," said Zoei. "Priel was with me but Ezekiel was so much bigger than him, so I yelled, 'Creator, please help us!' Then Mr U-ie was there in, like, two seconds. Then you came, and you were both fabulous and made the bad guy go away."

"Thank you, Zoei," said Michael. "Do all of you understand what Zoei did?"

"She called on the Creator before trying to do anything herself?" asked Ryan.

"Correct," said Michael. "All your powers and strategies are no match for the help you will get if you call on the Creator. Thank you, Zoei."

"No problem," she said and gave the angel a high five.

Roni put her hand up, like she was in school. "Michael, I tried to do what I saw you do. Hit my heart and tried to get a sword to appear. Why couldn't I do it?"

"Good question," said Michael. "If you were an Olympic swimmer, would you just show up at the Games without any preparation? No practice? No strength training? Of course not. Therefore you should not expect to be able to participate in spiritual warfare if you have not been properly trained."

"Spiritual warfare?" said Roni.

"The Creator laid it out very plainly in the Scriptures. Our struggle is not against flesh and blood, but against rulers, against the authorities, against the powers of this dark world, and against the spiritual forces of evil in the heavenly realms. The battle for the human soul is now being actively fought all around us.

"Your eyes have been opened to the spirit world. The Creator has chosen you as part of a bigger plan. A resistance to the Dark One's siege on the human soul. If you choose to commit to this far-reaching conflict, it will not be easy in any way. It may cost you your family, your friends, even your life.

"Let us begin training, as you consider your life hereafter. How many books are in the Bible?"

"Sixty-six," said Jeni.

"What books tell us about the Creator's time on Earth as a man?"

"The Gospels," said Juli. "Matthew, Mark, Luke and John."

"What book tells about the creation of all things?"

"Genesis!" shouted Zoei.

Roni thought back to when her mom had a Wednesday night Bible Study for kids. What great memories those were!

"Wait a minute, Michael," she said. "Our mom wrote the book when it comes to Bible questions. You're gonna have to do better than that when it comes to all things Bible." Everyone laughed.

"Alright, alright," Michael said. "Something harder, maybe something about the prophets? Which prophet said this?

> "The Spirit of the Lord GOD is upon me; because the LORD hath anointed me to preach good tidings unto the meek; he hath sent me to bind up the brokenhearted, to proclaim liberty to the captives, and the opening of the prison to them that are bound; To proclaim the acceptable year of the LORD, and the day of vengeance of our God."

Roni sat there waiting for one of the others to answer. She didn't like to come off as a know-it-all. It was quiet for at least a minute, then she spoke up.

"*Isaiah 61:1-2*," she said.

"Good," said Michael. "Now..."

"Excuse me, Michael," interrupted Ryan. "I thought you were going to teach us self-defense, not have a Bible quiz."

Michael thought for a moment. Then he said to Ryan, "Come, stand over here, in front of me."

Ryan obeyed.

"Now, draw your sword."

Ryan stood there, confused. "What sword?" he said.

"Exactly," said Michael.

The archangel hit his chest, right over his heart, and shouted, "The sword of the Lord!" Immediately a shining sword appeared in his hand.

"Wow!" Ryan jumped back.

"How did you do that?" asked Jeni.

"This is Adoni-Zedek, Lord of Justice," Michael said as he beheld the beautiful weapon. He put both hands on the golden hilt and cut through the air as if the silver blade could separate oxygen from carbon dioxide.

"The Creator says," Michael continued, "that his Word is living and active, sharper than any double-edged sword. In order for you to have a sword to use in spiritual warfare, you must have the living Word of the Creator in your heart."

"I see," said Roni.

Michael smiled at her and lowered Adoni-Zedek.

"Good. Now I would like you to spend the next hour training for battle. Start with Ephesians 6. I want you to understand the armor you will be wearing when you fight."

"Will we be practicing with our swords once we get them to appear?" asked Jeni.

"One thing at a time, Jeni. Please begin your training now. Zoei, Priel will help you," said Michael.

"Yay!" shouted Zoei. She ran over to Priel and jumped into his arms. He tossed her about five feet in the air and then caught her. Roni jumped out of her seat and Michael saw her distress.

"Priel, easy with the human," he said.

The guardian lowered the small child and apologized to Roni. "I have no desire to harm your sister. I would give my very *essentia* for her."

"Thank you," Roni said.

"You are welcome," Priel replied.

"Roni, Ryan, I would like to see both of you at the end of the hour, please," Michael said.

"Ok," they both replied.

Ryan went inside to look for the Bible that had belonged to Roni's dad. Roni stopped Michael before he could leave. It seemed that now was as good a time as any to talk to him.

"Wait, Michael," she said. "I just wanted to thank you for saving my sister's life and mine too. I know it was stupid of me to run out there so ill-prepared, but I couldn't have lived with myself if Zoei had died while I stood by and did nothing."

Michael looked at this extraordinary human girl standing before him. So much passion and zeal bottled up in one person. It was no wonder why Ezekiel wanted her and why the Creator was willing to go to such great lengths to protect her.

"I want to tell you a story, Roni. It's about a young orphan girl. She was born to a captive people that were living in a wealthy, godless land. She was taken away from her family to become the most unlikely winner of a beauty contest. And the prize for this contest was marriage to the king of this godless land.

"She had no idea why she was chosen for this role until one day a wicked man demanded the annihilation of her people. The only way to save them was to go unannounced before her husband and king and plead for her life and the life of her people. However, it was illegal for her to do this, and she was afraid.

"Her uncle, her only living relative, sent her a message and it said something like this: 'Do not imagine that you, in the king's palace, can escape any more than the rest of us. For if you remain silent, help for your people will come from another place, but you and your father's house will perish.' But then he ended it with a phrase I want you to remember. He said, '...and who knows whether you have attained royalty for such a time as this?'"

He paused for a moment and then said, "I know you did not ask for this battle against the Dark One, but you *are* involved. You must make a choice."

"I know this story," Roni said. "It's about Esther. She was a Jew who became the queen of all Persia."

"You are right, and do you remember what she did after she received the message?"

"She fasted and prayed for three days and then she went to the king."

"Indeed, she had attained royalty in order to save her people." He reached out and touched Roni's cheek. "Who knows, Miss Roni Susan Chambers, perhaps you have been born for such a time as this?"

Roni blushed. "But I don't really know what to do," she replied.

"You are one of the bravest humans I know. Ezekiel would exploit your gifts for his own selfish purposes. You were strong to back away from him; he can be very intimidating. I understand why you ran to help Zoei. Just remember, you don't have to win every battle on your own. Call on the Creator. He will fight for you."

Roni felt encouraged. She curled up on the end of the couch and opened her Bible to the passage Michael had requested them to read. She tried to imagine herself in the pieces of armor laid out in Ephesians 6.

> Finally, be strong in the Lord and in his mighty power. Put on the full armor of God so that you can take your stand against the devil's schemes. For our struggle is not against flesh and blood, but against the rulers, against the authorities, against the powers of this dark world and against the spiritual forces of evil in the heavenly realms.
>
> Therefore put on the full armor of God, so that when the day of evil comes, you may be able to stand your ground, and after you have done everything, to stand. Stand firm then, with the belt of truth buckled around your waist, with the breastplate of righteousness in place, and with your feet fitted with the readiness that comes from the gospel of peace. In addition to all this, take up the shield of faith, with which you can extinguish all the flaming arrows of the evil one. Take the helmet of salvation and the sword of the Spirit, which is the word of God.
>
> *Ephesians 6:10-17, NIV*

CHAPTER 14

Surprises

*"For we wrestle not against flesh and blood, but
against principalities, against powers, against the
rulers of the darkness of this world, against
spiritual wickedness in high places."*

Ephesians 6:12

Ryan and Roni made their way down to the basement again after the training session was over.

"What did you think of all the pieces of armor in Ephesians 6?" asked Ryan. "I thought I saw each one on Michael and Uriel when they were fighting with Ezekiel, except for the shield."

"When I read those verses," Roni replied, "I wondered if we would be wearing that kind of armor when we engage in battle."

"Me too!" exclaimed Ryan. "I've never been the Lord of the Rings type, but what I saw and read today may have won me over."

Both Roni and Ryan had a brilliance about them. The reading of the Scriptures had already begun to affect them. Michael was waiting for them at the little table in the corner. He noticed the change in both of them and rejoiced inwardly.

"How did your training go?" he asked.

"Fine," they both replied.

"Good. I want to continue where we left off this morning. Also, because the Dark One knows our location, I am going to have to give you some information that I was originally going to let you discover on your own. Before we begin, however, I want to say this: Roni, I'm not sure as to the extent of your powers yet. Have you had time to do anymore translation on the research, Ryan?"

"Not yet. I was hoping to get to it soon, now that Jeni is here. It does seem that I am still unable to heal the wound that was left on Roni's hand, though."

"Ok, I want you and Jeni to begin as soon as possible. We need to know what we are protecting."

"Yes, Michael."

"Now, there is something I need to tell both of you; something that may help you in your research. I told you that the Dark One's goal is to destroy the human soul, and once again he is trying to produce artificial life forms and genetically enhanced beings at an accelerated rate. It therefore only makes sense that he would utilize women's natural ability to carry multiple children at one time. So it should not come as a surprise when I tell you that you are twins."

Ryan of course wasn't surprised at this news about himself, but he looked at Roni, who appeared to be stunned.

"I don't have a twin," she said. "I was adopted by myself."

"Do you know that you and Jason and Ryan all left Russia on the same day?"

"Well, I know we all arrived in Kansas on the same night. Our parents told us that story a million times," she replied.

"And we all have the same birthday, March 27th," Ryan added.

"There was a mix-up when the three of you were shipped out, and the courier tried to fix the problem before you were delivered to your parents," Michael explained. "The Miller family was supposed to be receiving a set of twin boys and the Chambers family was supposed to get a little girl. However, the orphanage sent a little boy and a set of boy-girl twins. Roni, Jason was your twin brother, but he was put with the Millers because the orphanage made a mistake."

Roni couldn't believe what she was hearing. *She had a brother. Her sisters had a brother. Jason was their brother.* She sat there stunned, her thoughts racing. A flood of emotions was sweeping over the landscape of her mind, rearranging every hill and valley. This new surge of information was altering everything else in her life.

"I've got to go," she said abruptly and got up and walked away.

Ryan was speechless. His mind was spinning.

"Ryan," Michael continued, "your twin is a girl. Her name is China. She was adopted by another person here in Kansas and is being held against her will. And, now that the enemy knows where we are, she may end up being killed before we can get to her."

Ryan looked at Michael in disbelief. He felt like he was on new information overload. "This must be the way Roni has been feeling over the last month," he thought.

"China is a slave," said Michael.

"What? What... kind of slave?" Ryan asked. He really didn't need to ask; he already knew the answer.

"She was sold as a slave to a man named Joseph Cardian when she was eight years old. She was born with a cleft lip, so the people responsible for her existence did not want her for breeding purposes. They kept her for a while, then made some money by selling her. There are many children who are victims in the human trafficking business, who come from these evil monsters."

Ryan was still in a daze, trying to take in the news that he even had a sister; but to hear of her abuse was even more shocking. "Can we go get her?" he asked.

"That is why I have spoken of it to you. I am organizing a rescue party to go and get her. You and I, plus a few others, will leave in a week's time. I need you to ready yourself for spiritual warfare as much as you can by then."

"Why spiritual warfare? Are there evil angels guarding her?" Ryan asked.

"Most likely," Michael replied. "I have also learned that not only is the man a customer but he is also a dealer. Many young children go through this man's property on a weekly basis. We need to shut him down."

Ryan's heart was beating rapidly now. His face was beginning to turn red. Michael placed his hand on the young man's shoulder.

"Do not let your anger and hatred blind you to what we need to do. We are not to serve justice on Joseph. That is for the Creator to do," he cautioned gently. "There are three more boys and a girl in this area that are a result of selective breeding. The Evil One will be going after them as well, if he gets the chance. I have several angels out there, convincing them to come and aid us here. Their adoptive parents are being taken to a secret location so no harm can come to them."

Ryan hadn't even thought of his parents. The color began to leave his face. "My parents..."

"Are safe," Michael finished his sentence. "We moved them when we got the girls. They love you and miss you. I hope you will make a point of trying to reunite with them soon."

"I will. Tell me, how come there are so many of us out here in nowheresville Kansas?"

Michael looked at Ryan in silence, and he figured out the answer for himself.

"Because it's nowheresville Kansas."

"I believe I know the reason we found AIRborn technologies in, as you say, nowheresville Russia," said Michael. "Experimenting in a place with a high child-mortality rate would be a great cover up for failed research."

"That does make sense," said Ryan.

They sat quietly for a while, then Ryan stood up.

"I should go find Roni."

"Yes, you should," said Michael. "And Ryan..."

"Yes?"

"Do not try to fix it. Just listen."

***

Roni could hardly catch her breath. She had run through the house, up the stairs, into her parents' bedroom, and out onto the balcony. She lay down on her mother's porch swing.

Jason was her *brother?* She could hardly believe it; yet she felt like she had known it all along. Jason and Ryan looked and acted nothing alike. She wondered if Jason had the same nanites in his blood that she had in hers. If he did have them, why was he so young when he died? *Why am I still alive?* She touched her chest. She could feel the pacemaker working, and she wondered if this machine could have saved Jason.

She looked out at the horizon. She could see where the earth and sky met and remembered what her mom had said about heaven. She wondered if her parents were looking down on her from heaven or if that was even possible. She took hold of her necklace. Michael's words resonated in her mind. *Perhaps you were born for such a time as this.*

Born for what time? She lay on the swing for a while, hoping that perhaps if she waited long enough the voice that had come to her before would speak to her again. She lost all track of time...

The sun was setting when she felt someone sit down by her head. It was Ryan. He covered her with a blanket. She lifted her head and laid it on his lap. He stroked her head, like her mother used to do. They watched the sun go down.

Roni fell asleep.

CHAPTER 15

Slaves

"O Lord, how long will you look on? Rescue my life from their ravages, my precious life from these lions."

Psalm 35:17, NIV

Tuesday 5th November

BANG!

China jumped as the door at the top of the stairs was pushed open and hit the wall.

"You're just getting too fat to be of any use to me. I'll wait till you pop that kid out, and then we'll get back to having fun." Joseph's angry voice caused fear to rise in China. "I'll come for you later, China!"

Then the door slammed shut. China could hear Trinity crying at the top of the stairs. She walked up and took her hand, saying gently, "Come on, Trinity. You need your rest."

Trinity stood up and her bulging belly forced her to lean backward to keep her balance.

"Are you hurt?" China asked.

"Just my face," answered Trinity.

"I'll take a look at it when we get downstairs," she said with a very slight Russian accent.

The girls made their way downstairs carefully so Trinity wouldn't fall. China walked her to their bed and the pregnant girl sat down. One look at her friend's face and China knew that their master had hit her again.

She went to the refrigerator and made an ice pack for the girl's face.

"Want to tell me what happened?"

"Same thing as always; he got mad when I couldn't do what he wanted."

"How's the baby? Did he punch you again?'

"No, but..." Trinity started to cry. "He said he doesn't want to hurt the baby because he already has a buyer for it and..." She couldn't talk anymore, she was so upset.

"It's gonna be ok, Trinity."

But China knew it wasn't going to be ok. She had already been through the same ordeal twice. No one had been with her when it was her time. Both of her babies were stillborn, so at least she knew they weren't out somewhere in the world, suffering abuse. If Trinity's baby was born alive, they would both have the agony of the lost child being at the mercy of monsters like Joseph. He had laid off the beatings and renting Trinity out, so there was a high chance of the baby being born alive.

"Are all men as evil as Joseph and the men he loans me to?" China wondered. They must be. She had never met a nice one.

She loved Trinity. They had each other. They would tend to each other's wounds and then sleep safely in each other's arms until Joseph wanted them.

China had been born in a small room in Russia. With blond hair and blue eyes, she was just what the researchers at the facility wanted—but she had a flaw. She was born with a cleft lip, so she was not to be adopted out, like the other children born in the facility. She had a quick operation done when she was three months old, but the surgery was not carried out correctly, so her smile was permanently damaged. She didn't have much to smile about, anyway.

She was allowed to stay at the facility for a while. An elderly nurse took care of her. She named her China because she said she was like a beautiful china teacup with a small crack in it. By the time she was eight, the facility had begun to shut down. Her nurse had died by then, and she was shipped off to the United States—where the nightmare she had thought she lived in would seem like paradise compared to what her life became, living with Joseph.

He was a short, muscular man with small eyes and a sinister smile. His face, which was never clean shaven, had a redness to it that intensified when he was angry. He bought her for a few thousand dollars and took her home. Her eight-year-old innocence was stolen and she became nothing more than a ragdoll to an evil monster.

Joseph lived in a large ranch-style house in the country. It was a beautiful place. If she behaved, he would allow her to go outside. Once he had even let her ride a horse. There were a lot of animals to see and flowers to smell. It was nice to feel the fresh air. When she was ten, Joseph had given her a kitten. She loved the kitten and treasured it. But, by the time she was thirteen, Joseph had become tired of her. He stopped being nice to her. He made her cat stay outside and she couldn't go out of the house very much. By the time she was sixteen, she had become pregnant twice and given birth to two stillborn babies. That was when Joseph brought Trinity home.

Trinity was fourteen but very small for her age. She had blue eyes and dark brown hair that hung in perfect ringlets around her face. Her teeth were white and straight, and she had the most beautiful smile. The girls loved each other at once and became a shelter for one another.

After Trinity arrived, the girls were rented out to men more and more. There were a lot more children that came through the house too. Boys and girls. Last spring Trinity had discovered she was pregnant. After Joseph had beaten her, he told her she had better not lose the baby or he would rent her out permanently.

Trinity was just about due to deliver her baby, and China was getting nervous. She had delivered her babies alone, so she knew the pain her friend was in for. She didn't know whether to hope that the baby would live or die.

She paced the floor as she watched Trinity sleep. She looked around their room. The walls were just grey cinder blocks. The one window they had was made of glass blocks. It didn't even have a curtain. A washer and dryer were in a little room under the steps. Joseph made the girls do all the laundry for the house.

Trinity looked small and vulnerable as she slept on the king-size bed. China hated that bed. Both her children had died there and, before Trinity came, Joseph had spent many nights in it with her.

It was all so hopeless. There was nobody in the world who cared if they lived or died—let alone about Trinity's baby. She heard Joseph's heavy footsteps across the floor above her, then he was unbolting the slide lock on the door. Her heart sank.

"China, get up here," Joseph called. "I got someone I want you to meet."

It was two days before China came back to the room. Trinity looked at her but knew better than to ask any questions. China went into the bathroom and tried to remove her clothing carefully. She didn't want to pull too hard where her clothes were stuck to her body. Blood from her wounds had dried and adhered to her clothing. She cried out and Trinity came to the bathroom door.

"China, can I help you?"

"No, I'm fine," she lied, trying to sound like nothing was wrong.

"China, let me in. I know you need me."

The door opened slowly. Trinity came in. She saw China sitting on the toilet lid with her back to the door.

"I... I can't get my shirt off. It's too stuck on," she said, still trying to be brave.

"Let me see. What did he use?"

"They used a whip."

Trinity knew that this was going to be bad. A whip is terrible. It opens up hundreds of tiny scratches all over your body; then, when you put your clothes on, the blood dries, causing the fabric to stick to your skin. It looked like she had been dressed and undressed several times. This was the worst either of them had ever seen.

She tried several times to take China's clothes off but had to stop because the pain was more than the girl could bear. They knew they had to be quiet or Joseph would come down and beat them both. Finally Trinity suggested that she get in the shower with her clothes on and let the water soften the dried blood. That worked, but it still took more than half an hour to get the clothes off. Joseph must have passed out drunk or he would have come down and punished them for using up all the hot water.

China was covered in little whip marks from her neck to her feet. All they could think to do was to put petroleum jelly on the wounds, so the blood wouldn't reach the sheets. She would have to sleep with no clothes on, not even a blanket to cover her.

"I'll be right on the couch if you need me, China," she said, kissing her friend on the forehead. Then she asked, "Did you know the other man who was with Joseph?"

"His name was Ezekiel."

CHAPTER 16

Friends—and a Foe

"Proclaim ye this among the Gentiles; Prepare war,
wake up the mighty men, let all the men of war draw
near; let them come up: Beat your plowshares into
swords and your pruninghooks into spears:
let the weak say, I am strong."

Joel 3:9-10

Tuesday 5th November—Friday 8th November

Over the next two days Ryan trained all morning and in the afternoons worked on translating the research papers. Then it was back to training in the evenings. He was indefatigable. Due to his selective breeding, he could work very long hours and needed only four hours of sleep a day. Jeni too was able to match his resilience.

He spent many hours with Oriel, discussing the Scriptures, and was beginning to feel his spiritual strength growing. He talked to Roni about some of the other things that Michael had shared with him. They talked about his twin sister. Both were fearful for China and prayed fervently for her protection.

On the third day, after his training session in the morning, Ryan settled down with Jeni to continue poring over the research papers. They were finally getting somewhere. Jeni brought a large piece of paper over to where Ryan was working.

"This here looks like a huge math problem. Did you happen to bring a math genius with you?"

"I'm supposed to be the math genius here," said Ryan, "but I can't make head or tail of it. This is a medical formula that I translated back in Germany. It's how I figured out what to put into Roni's injections. I think this page tells how to reprogram the nanites to cause her to age properly."

"I think, when you gave Roni that electric shock at the football field, you automatically activated her electronic system," said Jeni.

"Yeah, maybe," said Ryan absently. He was frowning over a piece of research that was difficult to translate.

"It seems weird to talk about my sister like she is a computer."

"She's not a computer. Her mind is her own. It looks here like the researchers were able to tap into some of the... unused portions of her... brain. Wow! Jeni, what number does this look like?"

"Um... maybe 80 or 89. Why?"

"If we have translated this right, then Roni should potentially be able to access almost 80 percent of her brain!" exclaimed Ryan. "Mix that with the nanotechnology and she could..."

"Could what?"

Ryan looked at Jeni. She wasn't sure if he was happy, afraid or angry.

"Do what, Ryan?"

"Almost anything that has to do with magnetism or electricity."

Jeni could definitely see fear in Ryan's eyes.

"Let's finish this. I don't want to start talking and not have all the answers I can possibly have for Roni."

They worked all afternoon and evening and into the early hours of the next day. Finally at about 5am Jeni had reached her limit.

"I gotta stop and rest, Ryan. You need to stop too. Go get a little shut-eye and we can start again in a few hours."

Ryan agreed. "I'll see you in a little while then."

Jeni went to the bedroom she was sharing with her two sisters. Zoei was sound asleep and snoring in the bed closest to the door. Priel was standing next to her, alert to every breath the little girl took. Juli was asleep as well, but she seemed to be dreaming. Ariel was standing over her, trying to soothe away whatever was making her restless. Jeni smiled at Samuel as the angel took his post next to her bed. She closed her eyes and was asleep in seconds. It felt like she had just closed her eyes when she was awakened by the sound of Juli thrashing around in her bed. Jeni crawled out of bed and went over to her sister.

"Juli, Juli," whispered Jeni, trying not to awaken Zoei. "Juli, wake up."

Juli opened her eyes part way. "What is it, Jeni? I'm trying to sleep."

"So am I, but you're making too much of a racket."

"Sorry. I'll try to keep it down to a dull roar," Juli yawned and fell back asleep.

"Well, I'm glad someone can sleep," said Jeni to herself. She looked over and saw that Zoei was already up. She noticed the clock. It was almost 9am. She decided she might as well get up. She brushed her teeth, then went down into the kitchen.

"Morning, sleepyhead," said Roni. "You and Ryan been burning the midnight oil again? Well that genetic 'enhancement' you two got going looks like it's catching up on you. I believe a nap will be in order later today. Where's Juli?"

"She's still sleeping. Guess she had a rough night. Ariel is watching over her."

Just then, Ryan and three very attractive boys walked into the kitchen. Jeni froze.

"Hey, Jeni. Glad you're up. I got us some more help. I'd like you to meet Jared. He has an eidetic memory."

Jeni smiled sweetly and tried to smooth her unruly hair a bit. Then she realized she was still in her pajamas. Her face went a little red.

"Oh, great," she thought. "An eidetic memory. That means he'll always remember that the first time he met me I looked like a pile of wrinkled laundry with red hair. Note to self—kill Ryan later."

"I'm so happy to meet you, Miss," said Jared politely as he offered her his hand.

Everyone but Jeni could see that Jared was instantly taken with her. She extended her hand.

"Thank you. Sorry I'm not exactly dressed for company," she said apologetically, but Jared interrupted her.

"You look like an early morning sunrise," he smiled at her. "Just beautiful."

"Ah, sorry to interrupt, but this is Jared's sister," said Ryan.

Jeni looked over to where Ryan was pointing and saw the most stunning, well-dressed young woman she had ever seen. Long blond hair and striking blue eyes. Tall and thin, with fair skin. And, Jeni noticed, no freckles. She was a little jealous.

"I'm Jillian," said the young woman.

"I'm Jeni," she replied. She wanted to shake hands with Jillian but Jared had not let go her hand.

"Jared, maybe you should let her hand go," said his sister.

"Never."

"Jared," said Jillian a little firmer.

106

Jared finally let her hand go, but only after she agreed to have lunch with him. Jeni thought he was cute for a city boy. Blond hair and blue eyes like his sister. Tall and muscular, nicely tanned. Jeans and a red polo shirt. Her heart was taken.

Ryan interrupted her thoughts. "This is Seth and his twin brother Solomon," he said, introducing the pair of farm boys.

Seth and Solomon were obviously identical twins. Both were dressed in blue jeans, t-shirts and cowboy boots, but here the similarity ended. Their appearance clearly indicated that each boy had his own individual identity. Seth's hair was short and neat, while Solomon's was long and wavy and pulled back in a ponytail.

Solomon's forearms were covered in sleeve tattoos that looked like flames. As a child, he had saved his brother from a grass fire but burned his arms in the process. When he turned sixteen, his parents had allowed him to cover the scars with tattoos. Jeni noticed a scar above Seth's left eye. He had been kicked in the head by a young bull while trying to administer the animal's vaccines. He had nearly died but somehow pulled through with no brain damage.

Jeni looked at her hair, which was in a long braid. "How did Juli and I end up with red hair? And of course, I had to have green eyes instead of blue," she thought.

"Stupid genetics," she mumbled under her breath.

"What was that, Jeni?" asked Roni. She could sense that her little sister was feeling out of place with her looks.

Jeni was fiddling with her necklace. "Um... I was... uh... wondering how old these guys are," Jeni blurted out.

"My brother and I just turned seventeen last week," said Jillian.

"We are sixteen," said Seth.

"Oh... Ok... my sister Juli and I are sixteen too," Jeni smiled nervously.

"Alright, who's hungry?" Priscilla asked. "I'm sure these big boys need to eat, unless you're all angels?"

"I think I can speak for all the humans in the room. We will eat whatever you make," said Ryan, and he kissed Priscilla on the cheek.

Everyone voiced their agreement with Ryan.

"Well, get on out of here so we can get cooking," Priscilla ordered.

"We all just kinda do whatever she says," Roni informed their guests. "It's just easier that way. Don't worry, you won't regret it."

Roni hadn't noticed it, but she was holding onto her necklace. She looked over to Jeni, who was doing the same. They just kept staring at each other.

"What's wrong?" asked Ryan, when he noticed what was going on between the sisters.

"Something's wrong," said Jeni softly.

"I know," Roni whispered back.

"What is it?" inquired Ryan. "Quiet, everyone!"

Everyone in the house was quiet at once. A faint sound could be heard humming throughout all the rooms. Roni and Ryan tried to figure out where it was coming from.

Suddenly Zoei ran into the room. "Where is she?" she cried.

"Who?" asked Solomon.

Instantly, all three sisters knew! But it was Jeni who began to scream.

"Juli! It's Juli, Roni!"

Everyone sprinted up the stairs and ran toward the bedroom. The music was getting louder as they approached the room. They couldn't open the door, so Jeni began kicking and hitting it.

"Juli, I'm coming!" she shouted in desperation.

"Look out!" said Ryan, and he tried to push the door in. It wouldn't budge. Suddenly he remembered his training.

"The sword of the Lord!" he shouted.

A blaze of light filled the hallway and Ryan was dressed like Michael and Uriel when they were fighting Ezekiel. He held a brilliant sword in his hand. He was startled for a moment, but then he looked into Roni's tear-filled eyes. She grabbed his arm.

"In the name of the Lord," she whispered to him.

He nodded, and the girls backed away. Ryan swung his sword at the door and it splintered away like it was made of toothpicks.

He stepped into the room and saw Juli on her back, levitating about five feet above the floor. She was still alive and conscious. Her red hair and nightgown whipped around her body as if she was caught in a great torrent of wind. It looked like she was screaming, but the music was so loud no one could hear her. Tears were streaming down her face. She saw Ryan come into the room and she reached out to him. He looked back at her and tried to let her know that he was there for her.

Beyond Juli's bed he could see Ariel, battle axe in hand, fighting with a much larger angel that had a flaming red sword. The battle was so fierce that the humans could barely see the weapons cutting the air.

"Creator, I need help!" Ryan yelled toward the ceiling in the room.

At once Jared and Jillian came through the door dressed in their armor. Jillian wielded a sword similar to Ryan's, and Jared had two shorter swords drawn and ready for a fight. They immediately charged at the dark angel Ariel was fighting.

Ryan joined in the fight. The battle raged on for what seemed like an eternity, but in reality was less than five minutes. The three humans took over from Ariel, who was weakening. She had been battling all morning. They pushed the dark angel back into a corner and eventually out the window, where Uriel and Michael bound him up.

As the demon fell out the window, his power over Juli dissolved. The music faded away and she fell to the floor. Roni and Jeni ran over to her. She was delirious and mumbling to herself. The sisters lifted her back onto her bed. Ryan rushed to her side, his armor and sword disappearing as he knelt down. He laid his hand on her chest to check her respiration. Her heart was beating fast but it was gradually slowing down to normal.

"I'll have to get my medical bag, but she seems to be coming around."

He left the room to get his things and saw Michael talking to the apprehended demon. It was apparent that the intruder was not going cooperate.

"What do you want with Juli?" Ryan marched over and demanded of the infiltrator.

The rogue angel smirked at Ryan, for he had accomplished his task. Ryan was furious.

He shouted, "The sword of the Lord!" and his weapon appeared in his hand. He put the tip of his sword to the throat of the mocking prisoner.

"Ryan," Michael spoke in a smooth, calm voice. "It is not for us to deliver this rogue's punishment. That right belongs to the Creator. Put your sword away."

Ryan stood there for another minute. The prisoner continued to look amused at the discomfort he was bringing. "Do it," he taunted, "You know you want to. Let your anger out. I feel it burning in you."

"No, Ryan. Put your weapon away."

Ryan obeyed Michael.

"I must take him to the holding area," Michael informed Ryan. "I will return tonight. Please continue with your studies."

"Yes sir," Ryan replied.

He made his way back to Juli's room. She was awake and talking.

"Does she remember what happened?" Ryan asked.

"She found a package in the mailbox yesterday," said Roni. It contained a jump drive with music in it. It was addressed to her from Sharleen Miller. She loaded it onto her iPod and fell asleep with it in her ears. It contained an encrypted message as well as a summons to the evil angel."

"What was the message?"

Juli looked up at Ryan with her big blue eyes and said, "We are all going to die."

CHAPTER 17

To the Rescue

"Where then is my hope?
Who can see any hope for me?"

Job 17:15, NIV

Friday 8th November

"China, China, wake up. Something's happening!" Trinity tried to rouse her sleeping friend. "Wake up, China. Please!"

It had been almost 24 hours since China had crawled into bed after her two-day ordeal with Joseph and Ezekiel. Trinity had applied more petroleum jelly to the cuts on her body. She had a few deep lacerations around her neck. Trinity tried to clean and bandage them so they wouldn't get infected.

Trinity thought China was the most beautiful girl she had ever seen. With her fair skin and delicate features, she looked like an exquisite porcelain doll. It was sad that she had so many scars, and now Joseph had covered her whole body with whip marks. It would be a shame if the wounds left more scars.

She had held China's hand while her friend slept. Two long scars that ran from her wrists to halfway up both arms were a reminder of the children the sleeping girl had lost. She had almost succeeded in killing herself after the second baby was born dead. Trinity had been her lifesaver.

Now Trinity herself needed help.

"China!" she cried. "It's hurting... help me!"

China sat up and looked at her friend. Trinity was down on all fours, rocking back and forth. China knew at once what was happening.

"It's gonna be all right, Trinity," said China as she jumped out of bed and put some clothes on. Her whole body ached from the beatings and whipping she had suffered two days earlier, but she had to put the pain out of her mind for now. Trinity needed her. She went over to the frightened girl and knelt down beside her.

"Just try and breathe slowly. In and out, in and out," coached China.

After the contraction had eased a little, Trinity sat up. "Is the whole thing going to be like this?" she asked.

"I'm afraid so."

"Oh... Oh... the pain... it's killing me..." Trinity started to cry. "What do I do?"

"We just have to keep going and try to make it the best we can. Don't worry. I won't leave you."

**

Ryan waited up till Michael returned. Michael looked very uneasy as he walked into the kitchen. Ryan knew that there wasn't going to be any good news.

"The traitor has revealed the Dark One's intentions. We have to go tomorrow."

Ryan looked wide-eyed at Michael.

"Ok. What's the plan?"

"First, you must regain some of your strength. Go and sleep for a while. I will wake you in four hours," said Michael, as he turned and left the kitchen.

"Sleep?" Ryan said to himself. "How in the world am I supposed to sleep with all this... this... stuff going on around me? Roni, Jeni, Juli, Zoei, China, and all the new recruits too. I'm going to have to figure a way to get off the merry-go-round in my mind."

Once more he remembered the Creator. "I ask that you allow me to sleep in peace, so I can do your will," he prayed. Then he walked over to the couch and was asleep in mere minutes.

***

Trinity cried out in pain as the contractions began to build in strength. It had been five hours since she had begun labor. Joseph had come down several times to see how things were progressing. He was on the phone with the buyer, bartering for the price of the child. Eventually, Trinity's screams were so loud that he had to leave.

"You're doing fine, Trinity," said China, holding back her tears.

"How much longer?"

"Soon, honey, soon."

The truth was, China didn't know how long it would be. Her babies had been born more quickly, compared to what was happening to Trinity. She checked to see if the baby's head was coming out. It wasn't showing. She was beginning to think something might be horribly wrong.

***

Michael put his hand on Ryan's shoulder.

"Ryan. Wake up."

Ryan immediately opened his eyes.

"Come. We have work to do."

In the basement, all the young men and a few angels had assembled. Jared, Seth and Solomon looked eager to

114

join in the rescue operation. There were three other angels that Ryan didn't know. He figured they were the protectors for the new men. Quick introductions were made. Camiel was with Jared. Lorrel was with Seth. And Saffron was with Solomon. Ryan wasn't sure how he was going to keep all those names straight.

"Would it not be best to travel by night, sir, so the enemy may be somewhat surprised?" It was the protector Saffron who had spoken.

"She has a good point," thought Ryan.

"The enemy already knows we are coming. Any attack will be met with planned and calculated resistance," answered Michael. "Trying to out-think them will be the only way to defeat them."

"Then we should do the opposite of the logical thing to do?" asked Seth.

Everyone was silent as they tried to figure out what Seth had just said.

"Let me explain," said Seth. "It's logical to attack at night, so we do it in the day. It's crazy to try to come at them from the front, so we *do* attack them from the front. Do you see what I mean?"

"Yes," said Michael. "I do believe you are right."

The group of men and angels spent the next two hours putting together an attack-and-rescue plan.

"We leave at dawn," Michael announced. "Now, go and prepare yourselves for battle."

Ryan went over to the couch and picked up the Bible that had once belonged to Roni's dad. There was a black bookmark attached to the book, so he opened it up to the page it had marked. A passage in the Book of Psalms was highlighted on the right side of the page. He began to read. The words were beautiful, written in the old King James Version style. As Ryan read, he could see the words turning into beings and objects. He could see the *living* Word of God...

He that dwelleth in the secret place of the most High shall abide under the shadow of the Almighty. I will say of the LORD, He is my refuge and my fortress: my God; in him will I trust.

Surely he shall deliver thee from the snare of the fowler, and from the noisome pestilence. He shall cover thee with his feathers, and under his wings shalt thou trust: his truth shall be thy shield and buckler.

Thou shalt not be afraid for the terror by night; nor for the arrow that flieth by day; Nor for the pestilence that walketh in darkness; nor for the destruction that wasteth at noonday.

A thousand shall fall at thy side, and ten thousand at thy right hand; but it shall not come nigh thee. Only with thine eyes shalt thou behold and see the reward of the wicked.

Because thou hast made the LORD, which is my refuge, even the most High, thy habitation; there shall no evil befall thee, neither shall any plague come nigh thy dwelling.

For he shall give his angels charge over thee, to keep thee in all thy ways. They shall bear thee up in their hands, lest thou dash thy foot against a stone. Thou shalt tread upon the lion and adder: the young lion and the dragon shalt thou trample under feet.

> Because he hath set his love upon me, therefore will I deliver him: I will set him on high, because he hath known my name. He shall call upon me, and I will answer him: I will be with him in trouble; I will deliver him, and honor him. With long life will I satisfy him, and shew him my salvation.

Psalm 91

Ryan could feel the words sinking into his spirit. He could breathe them in. Touch them. As he meditated on them, the words put fresh heart into him. He felt that he could face anything in his way.

He sat with his eyes closed for a long time. When he opened them, Roni was sitting next to him. She looked as though she had been crying.

"What's the matter, Roni?" he said as he turned to face her.

"I know what you are going to do," she said and she leaned her head on his chest. "I want you to be careful and come back safe and... and..."

Roni began to cry uncontrollably. Ryan tried to comfort her but she seemed inconsolable. After a while, she composed herself and looked up at him. Her face was still red from crying.

"I just want you to know that I do forgive you for leaving me with Jason and for the way you treated us. We were just kids. How could you have known what would happen?"

Now it was Ryan's turn to cry. He hugged her and kissed her forehead. She had said the words he longed to hear. He had never been so happy.

"I want you to wear this when you go to get your sister," said Roni, and she held out her crystal necklace to him. "Let it remind you that someone here is praying for you."

"Thank you," was all he could say as he took the necklace from her. He knew the significance of the piece of jewelry she had given to him. It was the ultimate symbol of Roni's love for her dead parents, and she was giving it to him.

"It will bring you back to me," said Roni. She hugged him tightly once more. Then she walked away.

CHAPTER 18

A Cry for Help

*"In my distress I called upon the LORD, and cried
unto my God: he heard my voice out of his temple,
and my cry came before him, even into his ears."*

Psalm 18:6

Saturday 9th November

All night Trinity labored. She found only small relief between the ever mounting contractions. China tried to keep her comfortable but it was getting more and more difficult. In the morning Joseph came down again, hoping for an end result much quicker than Trinity could give.

"Hurry up, you worthless piece of trash, or I'm gonna give all three of you to Ezekiel and start over with some fresh girls," he bellowed. "And, if you think he will be kinder than me, ha! You've got another think coming!"

"She can't go any faster than she is! Stop yelling at her!" screamed China.

Joseph hit her hard across the face, bloodying her lip and opening up the wound on her neck again.

"You've gotten far too cocky for an ugly little whore! Deliver this child alive, or you're gonna be wishing you were dead. If you think the whipping you just got was bad..." with this ominous threat, he stormed up the stairs and slammed the door behind him.

"Please try, Trinity!"

"I can't do this anymore. I'm so tired," she whispered. She laid her head on China, as though she could take a long nap, but within thirty seconds another contraction enveloped her body and she cried out again.

China didn't know what to do. She stroked Trinity's forehead, trying to soothe the exhausted girl. They had no one to turn to for help. In a moment of desperation, she cried out, "Somebody, please help us!"

In the same instant, a brilliant light filled the room and two shining people stood before her. A man so tall he almost touched the ceiling, and a woman more beautiful than anyone China had ever seen. Her hair was long and dark. It fell past her waist. Her skin was lovely and white, and she smelled of sweet Georgia peaches. China wanted to scream when she saw them but, when she opened her mouth, no sound came out.

"I am Neil and this is Anastasia. We have come to help you," said the man.

The woman knelt down on her knees beside Trinity and took the young girl in her arms. She cradled her as if she were an infant in need of its mother. She spoke gently to Trinity. "Yes, my child, you will be home soon. This pain cannot last for much longer now."

China began to feel a little weak in the knees and Neil caught her as she fell backward. Although she was afraid of him—for she had never known a kind man—she allowed him to pick her up and bring her to the bed. He laid her down gently and turned to find her something to drink.

"Who are you?" China asked as she took a sip of water.

"We are your guardians. You have asked for help, so we are here," said Neil.

"Where have you come from?" China asked. Her curiosity was heightened by this kind man with red hair. She reached up and touched his face. He wore a goatee and his eyes were blue like the sky.

"From heaven, child," said the woman.

China was so tired that she hadn't paid much attention to Trinity for the last fifteen minutes or so that the angels had been there. When she looked over at the woman, she noticed that Trinity had a look of peace on her face as she gazed into Anastasia's eyes.

For a moment China was happy. She thought the visitor had calmed her friend down and the baby would be born soon. Then she looked down at the bed and saw a puddle of blood pooling at the woman's knees.

"TRINITY!"

**

The group of men and angels had made the trip to Joseph's ranch quite easily. It was located only thirty minutes from the Chambers' lake house. When they arrived, they were surprised to find everything quiet. Seth and Lorrel checked out the barn, expecting to find a squad of enemy soldiers ready to fight. But there were none. To the east of the house was a corn field that nobody had bothered to harvest. Everyone took cover in the field and waited to see what was going on. Their plan of a full frontal assault seemed to be on hold.

About half an hour later, a blue minivan pulled up at the house. A young, well-dressed man stepped out. Joseph came out of the house and greeted him with a handshake. They both walked over to the back door of the van and looked through the glass. Joseph seemed very pleased with what he saw. Both men made their way to the porch. They sat down and talked for a while. It was apparent that they knew one another well and had had past meetings together.

After fifteen minutes or so, they appeared to have concluded their business. Joseph handed the younger man a large envelope which looked like it contained a lot of money. Looking well pleased, he went to the back of the van and opened the door. To the onlookers' horror, out tumbled two small boys who couldn't have been more than four years old. Both had the same blond hair and blue eyes as Ryan and the other young men.

"Oh, no. They didn't!" said Saffron under her breath.

From across the yard, they saw Seth and Lorrel approaching Joseph and his guest.

"Guess they agreed with Saffron," Solomon said.

"Let's wait and see what happens," said Michael.

Out of the corner of his eye, Ryan thought he saw a bright flash of light come from the bottom of the house. Michael saw it too, and he nodded as Ryan motioned to him that he wanted to check it out.

About twenty feet from the window stood a large tree with branches that nearly touched the ground. It provided enough cover for Ryan to reach the house without being seen by the men in the front yard.

He crawled on his belly to the house and then lay as still as possible. To his disappointment, what he thought was a window was merely glass blocks set into the foundation of the house. He peered through the glass, trying to see what was going on in the basement. He could make out the figure of a tall man. From his height, Ryan thought he must be an angel, but whether he was a good or evil one, the young man had no way of knowing. He could see the form of another angel in the room. It looked like she was sitting on the ground.

Just then, he heard a scream and saw the figure of a small human jumping up and trying to pull something out of the sitting angel's arms. The scream alarmed Ryan, and he got up from the ground and made a dash for the front door.

The scream had alarmed everyone in the yard as well. Seth and Lorrel were done talking with the men and had sat them both down in the dirt until they could be taken to Michael. Seth had tied their hands together with some twine he had found in the barn. Lorrel had taken the two little boys onto the porch and stood on guard, while Seth joined Ryan in the house.

Both young men searched the house with their swords in hand. Another scream was heard, and the two men made their way to the kitchen and found the door which led to the basement. It was barred with a large two-by-four that was easily removed. They slid the lock open as quietly as they could. Then the young men crept slowly down the stairs.

***

China was so busy trying to talk to Trinity that she did not notice the armored men making their way down the steps. Trinity was slipping away and nothing she could do would save her friend.

"No, no, no! You can't leave me, Trinity. I love you. You're all I have!" she cried, kissing the girl's face. Suddenly she felt a hand on her shoulder and heard a gentle voice speaking to her.

"Miss, please, I'm a doctor. Let me look at your friend." The voice belonged to a blond-haired, blue-eyed young man who couldn't have been much older than her.

He looked like a lot of the boys who had lived back in Russia at the facility where she was born. She gave him a frightened look and held on tighter to Trinity. Anastasia reached out and touched her hand. No words were spoken, but China knew the doctor meant them no harm. Slowly, she relinquished her hold on Trinity.

Ryan knelt down next to the exhausted girl. After he had examined Trinity, he spoke to China.

"I'm afraid your friend has what is called *placenta previa*. The organ that feeds the fetus has covered the place for the baby to come out. She has lost a very large amount of blood. I'm afraid she'll most likely not live."

Ryan had never had to say that before. The words stuck in his throat. He had been a research doctor for most of his career. The only patient he had ever had that almost died was Roni.

China looked at him, unable to speak. What was this man saying? She thought she heard him say that Trinity was going to die. *Trinity was going to die? No. this can't be. What would she do? Who would love her?*

She walked over to the bed again. There was so much blood. She sat down and looked at Trinity. Then she laid her head down on the pillow and put her arms around her friend.

"China," Trinity whispered. "It's ok. You can let me go. Ryan will take care of you."

"Ryan?" China was confused. "Who is Ryan? Trinity, what are you saying? Please don't leave me. I love you. I need you."

"The baby will need you. You have to be strong for her."

"I don't want the baby, I want you!"

"Anastasia will help you when she gets back."

"Back from where?" asked China, and she looked up at the angel's face. Anastasia was crying and smiling at the same time.

"She has to take me home to see my Father. He is waiting."

"What? You don't have a father, Trinity."

"Yes, I do. And so do you." Trinity smiled sweetly and reached her hand up to heaven.

And then she was gone.

CHAPTER 19

Safe at Last!

"But whoso shall offend one of these little ones which believe in me, it were better for him that a millstone were hanged about his neck, and that he were drowned in the depth of the sea."

Matthew 18:6

"No, Trinity, no!" cried China as she shook the small frame of her lifeless friend. She looked over to the place where Anastasia had been sitting, but she was gone. Despair filled the girl's heart. A lament like nothing Ryan or Seth had ever heard came from China's small, disfigured mouth. It sounded like her heart was splintering into a thousand pieces.

Neil came near, trying to comfort her, but she stood up and pushed him away, until his back was against the wall of her cell. When she could push him no farther, she began pounding on his chest with her small fists. Of course she couldn't hurt him, and he let her batter him until her strength was gone. Then she buried her head in her guardian's shirt and cried for her friend.

When her tears were gone, she walked back to Trinity's bed. She laid her head on her departed friend's chest. As she put her arm over Trinity, she felt something move in the dead girl's body, and she cried out in shock.

"It's the baby," cried Ryan, galvanized into action. "I can still save the baby!"

Neil tried to pull China away from Trinity's body, but she did not want to leave her friend. She struggled with the mighty angel for a few moments but, when she saw the doctor put a knife to Trinity's swollen belly, she fainted.

126

"Try and find me a little more light," Ryan said to Seth, who was standing back, dazed and awestruck at what he had just seen. One moment the angel had been there, and the next she wasn't.

"Seth!"

"Oh, ok!"

Seth ran upstairs and looked around the kitchen. He found a flashlight right next to the back door. He sprinted back downstairs and turned the light on and held it steadily for Ryan. The other angel was back. She was assisting in the delivery of the baby. Seth felt like fainting at the sight of so much blood. He was a farm boy and used to animal blood, but human blood was a different story.

"Steady, Seth," said Lorrel. He put his hand on the boy's shoulder, and immediately Seth felt stronger.

"Ok. The baby is out," said Ryan.

He cut the umbilical cord and tried to revive the baby. She was not responding. When he had tried everything he knew to get her to breathe, he turned to the Creator. He prayed a prayer of help and then placed his hands around the child's body. A soft, warm glow emanated from beneath his hands.

China was regaining consciousness. When she opened her eyes, she saw Ryan with his hands on the baby. She walked over to them and took the infant's tiny hand in her own. The light began to shine brighter. China looked down at her own hand and was shocked to see that the same light coming from the doctor's hands was coming from her hand as well. Ryan looked at her in amazement.

The baby began to move. All eyes were on her now, as the once lifeless body drew its first breath. The infant let out a cough and then a very loud cry. China immediately picked the child up and began to comfort her. After a few minutes, Ryan spoke to her.

"Have you thought of a name for the baby?"

China hadn't even thought of naming the child because she was supposed to be sold to someone.

"Not yet," she answered. "Who are you and how did you know where to find us?"

"Well, that's kind of a long story. Maybe we should clean up a bit and then we can talk." Ryan paused for a moment, then said, "I'm sorry I wasn't able to save your friend."

China looked over at the bed and a tear rolled down her face.

"Do not worry, child," said Anastasia. "She is happy now. She is with her Father. She is no longer in pain. You will see her again someday." She looked down at the baby. "May I hold my new charge?"

China held the baby close to her chest. "What do you mean, your new charge?"

"Now that her mother has gone to heaven, I have asked to be this little one's guardian," replied Anastasia, gazing lovingly at the tiny infant.

"Why does she need a guardian? She'll have me," China darted back at this person, who she felt was trying to steal this little part of Trinity from her. The only part she had left.

"Every child of the Creator has a guardian to help keep watch over them. You have Neil and now the baby has me."

China looked over at Neil. He smiled gently at her. She wasn't sure what to do. He looked at her with such kindness that she felt like she wanted to trust him; but her head was still protecting her heart.

Neil walked over to China and spoke to her. "Maybe Anastasia could hold the baby while you get cleaned up. I will try and find something for the child to eat."

China looked down at her blood-soaked clothing. The thought of being covered in Trinity's blood made her stomach lurch. She handed the baby over to Anastasia, went over to her closet and pulled out a well-worn pink dress. Then she went into the bathroom and closed the door. She got out of her soiled clothing and looked at herself in the mirror. Her whip marks were healing well, although her neck looked terrible. The scab had been ripped open the last time Joseph hit her. Dried blood was making the bandage stick terribly. She got in the shower and soaked it off. After she had washed her hair, she stood in the shower crying until the hot water ran out.

Outside the house, Michael and the other members of the rescue team were dealing with Joseph and the other man.

"I don't know who you are, but you had better release us, or else!" Joseph yelled at them. "I'm calling the cops! This is trespassing and kidnapping and..."

"Really?" said Camiel, looking down at the pathetic men. "You really want to call the police? Do you know what happens to men like you in prison? It would be better if a millstone were hung around your neck and you were thrown in the sea."

Joseph frowned at him.

"I am afraid that quoting the Creator to this creature is a waste of time, Camiel. He obviously has not read the words of our Master," said Michael.

Then, turning to the two men, he announced, "The police have been contacted and will be here within the hour. You two will soon be getting what you deserve. If you repent of your evil ways, perhaps the Creator will not make you pay in the afterlife too."

For the first time, a look of terror came upon the faces of the two men. The weight of their evil ways was upon them. They knew that no amount of pleading would get them mercy from their captors.

Michael talked to the little boys, James and John, who had almost been sold into a life of slavery. They seemed to be fine. They were unaware of the tragic life they had narrowly missed. The younger man, whose name was Victor Green, had made arrangements through Joseph to sell them to a customer in Wyoming. The boys' guardian angels, Clayton and Daniel, told Michael that the two children were orphans and had no family to return to.

"Then they will stay with us," said Michael.

Michael had worked with child services before. He had a contact—Madeline Grey, a social worker—who helped children get placed quickly with families. He would also talk to her about Trinity's baby. The police arrived and took the men into custody. Madeline went over the children's cases with Michael.

"We are entering a grey area of the law, Michael," she said. "I can't just keep putting children into your custody. The three children are going to need to be legally adopted by stable parents."

"Can I get temporary custody of them for now?"

"Yes," she replied, "but they need to be checked out at the hospital before I can release them to you. The infant will need to spend at least 24 hours there, to be monitored and to get a birth certificate and social security card issued."

"Very well," said Michael. "I know a doctor who works out of a hospital in Wichita. He will examine the children, if that is ok?"

"Sounds like a plan," Madeline said. She liked Michael. He was compassionate and understanding. "Wish we had more men like him," she thought.

Madeline had met Michael seven years earlier in a similar situation. Michael and some of his associates had discovered a child-trafficking ring working out of southeastern Kansas, and there were several children who needed immediate housing.

Foster homes had been on the decline for several years because of the stringent rules and regulations the state and federal governments had put on families willing to house displaced children. Time after time, prospective foster parents had to back out of their training—simply because the law required them to rip out their whole porch if it was two inches too high. Or the state wanted the foster parents to cause potential damage to the foundations of their homes because the basement windows were one inch too small.

Michael had been a godsend to Madeline. He always seemed to know where she could find potential homes with the perfect house specifications. Their placement percentages were almost perfect. She didn't know where Michael came from or who he worked for, but she worked hard to keep him and his associates' names off the books.

Not only was he the best-looking man Madeline had ever met, he was also the kindest and most thoughtful. She lay awake at night thinking about him. She hadn't seen a wedding band or a ring tan line on his finger. Probably too busy doing good... yes... that was it... too busy for a relationship, she thought. He was just like her, married to his work.

***

After the police had taken Joseph and Victor away, two ambulances came to the house. The first vehicle took Trinity's body to the coroner. The second was to take China and the baby to the hospital. James and John went off with Madeline in her car.

Ryan sat in the back of the ambulance with his sister. She needed to be treated for all the cuts on her body. And Ryan was going to order a full set of body x-rays and blood tests too. He figured she hadn't been to any kind of hospital since she came over from Russia. It was a long drive to the hospital, so there was plenty of time for them to talk together.

"I know you were wondering who your friend said was going to take care of you. Well, I'm Ryan and I'm your brother. I will take care of you, if you will let me."

He thought it would be best just to get all the information out at once and then let China ask questions.

"I didn't even know you existed until a few days ago. Michael found out where you were and we came to get you before a man named Ezekiel could harm you."

China cringed at the sound of the name. She looked directly into Ryan's eyes.

"You were too late."

"He was here?" asked Ryan. He was shocked.

"Where do you think I got all these marks from?" China said bitterly.

"I am so sorry, China," was all Ryan could say.

After about twenty minutes, China started asking Ryan questions.

"How do you know I'm your sister? I don't remember you at all."

"I was adopted when I was still an infant, so I suppose we wouldn't remember each other. Michael said the facility where we were born wouldn't let you be adopted because of your... um..." Ryan pointed to her mouth, trying not to embarrass her too much.

"It's ok. Just say it," said China. "I know my mouth is ugly."

"I wouldn't say it's ugly," said Ryan. "I know someone who could fix your lip if you wanted them to. There is a very nice plastic surgeon at the hospital we are going to. I could ask if she would at least come see you while we are there, if you want."

China looked at Ryan skeptically. "Why are you being so nice to me? What do you want? You're supposed to be my brother so... some things would be just..."

"No, no, no!" Ryan exclaimed. "It's not like that at all!"

"Poor girl!" thought Ryan. "The only bargaining chip she has ever had in her life has been her body!"

"Listen to me, China. That life is over for you. I want you to know that I will take care of you, not because you have something to give to me, but because you are my sister and I love you.

"We have parents too, that will love you. I called mom right after I found out about you, and she is so excited to meet you. Dad is too. As soon as they get to go back to the house, they are going to fix up a bedroom for you, and you can stay with us for as long as you want."

China sat quietly in disbelief, staring at this strange man. Wondering why he would offer her a family, a home, and love, without any payment. She had never had that kind of affection in her life.

Everything costs something. That was what she had learned from Joseph. Could this man be telling her the truth? Was there someone in the world that she could turn to? She wasn't sure how to respond to Ryan.

"Well... what about the baby? She isn't going anywhere without me."

"We can figure that out too. Michael knows a social worker that helps children... um... people like you and the baby."

It was quiet for a little while as China continued to wonder about Ryan.

"I'm sure that all this is very overwhelming right now," said Ryan, seeing the confusion on her face. "We can just take it one day at a time."

He smiled at her and gently took her hand in his. "I'm so glad I have found you."

CHAPTER 20

More than a Storm

*"Be sober, be vigilant; because your adversary
the devil, as a roaring lion, walketh about,
seeking whom he may devour."*

1 Peter 5:8

As soon as the rescue party left the lake house, the trouble began. Slowly at first, so nobody realized what was happening until it was almost too late.

Juli had spent the morning sleeping in. She was exhausted from her encounter the day before. Jeni, Ariel and Samuel never left her. All three stayed awake by her side and would not even hear of taking turns to watch over her.

Zoei was out on the balcony, playing with her dollhouse. Priel stood guard over her, intently watching the horizon for any sign of Ezekiel.

Uriel, Gabriel and Ralph walked the property continually, making sure the house and its precious occupants were safe. They discussed whether or not the others were walking into a trap. None of them had sensed any disturbances in the spiritual realm, and they weren't expecting any real trouble while Michael and the others were away.

Priscilla stood guard in the house, keeping her mind alert to the possibility of unwanted intruders. Like a watchful mother bear, she was determined to keep her cubs safe.

Jillian was in the yard, sparring with her guardian, Raven. She was such a princess, with her bouncy blond curls, professional-looking makeup, and designer clothes.

She looked like she belonged on the cover of a fashion magazine, but there was more to her than just a pretty face—much more. She was relentless when it came to fighting, as Roni had witnessed when Juli was being attacked.

Roni was in the kitchen, making lunch for everyone. Chicken and noodles with homemade bread seemed like a good meal for a chilly November day. As she rolled out the noodles, she remembered how her mother had taught her to make them. Two eggs. One cup of flour. Mom would roll out the dough and then let Roni cut it with the pizza cutter. She tried to get every strand of the noodles exactly the same. Roni smiled as she thought of those happy times.

"How's it going?"

Roni was so deep in thought that she didn't hear Jillian talking to her.

"Hello," said Jillian again. She had come into the kitchen to get a drink of water.

"Oh... hi... um... sorry," said Roni, stumbling over her words. "I just get zoned in on what I'm doing sometimes, and I don't hear anything."

"It's ok," replied Jillian. "That smells delish! What is it?"

"Just some homemade chicken and noodles," Roni replied, as she stirred the pot of chicken broth bubbling on the stove.

"Wow! I wish I could cook. I can barely boil water." Jillian laughed at her own shortcomings. Then she changed the subject. "I know you're worried about Ryan. How long have you two been dating?"

"Oh... well... we aren't together," said Roni nervously.

"Oh. My mistake," said Jillian. "He is cute but he reminds me too much of Jared. That would just be weird! So what do you do for fun?"

"Fun? I don't really remember having fun," said Roni. "My parents died last year and I got legal custody of my three younger sisters. I also tried to go back to school to finish out my senior year of high school, but that's not working out very well.

"I was captain of the cheerleaders but my heart ended up giving out on the football field... and I died at the homecoming game. So I think the last time I had fun was... maybe... two years ago."

"Wow! Sounds like you need a night out with your girlfriends," said Jillian.

Roni laughed out loud. "I'm not sure who you think I am, but I assure you I do not have girlfriends. I had a friend at school but she graduated with our class last year. She's off living her life and I'm stuck here playing Mommy Dearest."

Roni paused for a moment. "I'm having a pity party, I guess. Maybe, when life gets back to normal, I can have a night out."

Jillian smiled at her and said, "My mom was the oldest of eleven kids. Her mom died when she was just sixteen years old. She never got to have a lot of fun either, when she was young. When she married my dad, she just wanted a small family so they could do a lot more stuff; but then she found out that she couldn't have any children at all.

"I know she was devastated, but she prayed and asked God for just one child to love. She said God was generous when he sent me and my brother to her. She always tells us to be thankful for the crazy times in our life because we're going to miss them when they're gone."

Roni pondered what Jillian had said for a moment, and then replied, "That's good advice, Jillian. I'll keep that in mind."

Roni hadn't been watching the stove while she and Jillian were talking. The soup began to boil over and hot chicken broth was everywhere. Roni grabbed a towel with her burned hand.

"It never fails," she mumbled under her breath. "It always boil over when I make this soup."

As she started to wipe up the mess, the boiling broth reached her wound. Roni screamed from the pain. Jillian ran around the table and grabbed her hand. The pain in her hand seemed to lessen with Jillian's touch.

"How did you do that?" asked Roni. She was in shock at what she had just experienced.

"I'm not sure," said Jillian. "Ever since I was a kid I've been able to take pain away from injured people."

"Does it hurt you?" inquired Roni.

"Some, but I've learned to brace myself for it. Jared can do it too. We have to be careful, though. If we take on too much pain, we can lose consciousness. Then we will be of no use to anybody," she said, laughing a little.

Roni wondered how this girl could laugh in the face of pain and even run to it. Priscilla came rushing into the room.

"Alright! What have you done this time, child?"

"Just aggravated my burn again," said Roni. "I'm ok, but I could use some more burn cream and fresh bandages."

"I'll tell you what's aggravating," said Priscilla. "You and your talent for hurting yourself. You're driving me nuts, child!"

The girls giggled a little at the angel's hysteria.

"What are you all worked up about, Priscilla?" inquired Ralph, who had just come back from another sweep of the grounds. "Are we going to be up all night listening to all the ways your charge got herself hurt today? I thought Gabriel was in here scaring the skin off some unsuspecting human again."

"I heard that," said Gabriel, who was right behind him. "And, as I recall, I wasn't the one getting Yoo-hoo spat all over himself the other morning."

Uriel and Raven came inside too.

"It's starting to rain out there," said Raven. "Sorry, Jillian, no more swordplay for today—unless Priscilla will let us go at it in the house."

Raven was a good name for this angel. His hair was jet black and it feathered back, just like a bird's wings. He was a bit of a prankster too, playing tricks on the more uptight angels. But you would never see him playing a prank on Michael; he did have some common sense. He was unmatched when it came to a sword fight and had taught Jillian to use her dueling skills in a very efficient way, by striking the heaviest blows with the least amount of energy.

"Don't even think of it," said Priscilla. "If you wake that baby upstairs, there will be no cinnamon rolls for you or your charge."

Just then Zoei and Priel came into the kitchen.

"Roni, did you boil the soup over again? She does that every time she makes chicken and noodles," she said to Priel, who just smiled. "She's just not a fabulous soup maker."

"Yes, Zo Bear, I did let the soup boil over again," Roni said, as she picked the girl up and began to tickle her. "Who's your favorite sister?"

"You, you, you!" squealed Zoei.

All of a sudden a loud clap of thunder was heard outside. It was almost deafening. Zoei screamed and covered her ears. She buried her head in Roni's chest.

"Careful, Zoei," said Roni. "My scar still hurts a bit. Can you go to Priel for now, while I go and make sure all the windows are closed?"

Zoei nodded and reached out to Priel.

"I will keep you safe, little one," said Priel gently to the child.

***

For the first few hours, the rain fell steadily. It wasn't raining heavily, but it was enough to saturate the ground and make any normal human being miserable if they had to be outside in it. Roni wasn't sure how the Watchers outside could stand it.

"They have been doing this for thousands of years," she thought. "They must be used to it by now."

She watched out the window for an hour or two, hoping to spot a ray of sunshine somewhere out on the horizon. Finally she gave up.

"Kansas weather, yuck," she muttered.

She went downstairs and saw Gabriel standing at his post in the living room. He had a slight frown on his face, as if he was contemplating something important. She didn't want to disturb him, so she quietly sat down and picked up a book that was lying on the couch. It was her father's Bible. The one she had let Ryan use. She leafed through the pages and found herself looking at the Book of Psalms.

"Psalm 121 is one of my favorites," said Gabriel.

She looked up at him, smiled, and flipped over a few pages to the passage. She began to read it out.

"I will lift up mine eyes unto the hills, from whence cometh my help. My help cometh from the LORD, which made heaven and earth.

He will not suffer thy foot to be moved: he that keepeth thee will not slumber. Behold, he that keepeth Israel shall neither slumber nor sleep.

The Lord is thy keeper: the LORD is thy shade upon thy right hand. The sun shall not smite thee by day, nor the moon by night.

The LORD shall preserve thee from all evil: he shall preserve thy soul. The LORD shall preserve thy going out and thy coming in from this time forth, and even for evermore."

Psalm 121

Roni drank in the beauty of the words. Was the Lord helping Ryan right now? Was he safe? She reached for her necklace but it was not there. Question after question kept rolling around in her mind until she thought she was going to go crazy, so she decided to distract herself.

"Excuse me, Gabriel," said Roni. "I was just wondering, what's the difference between a Watcher and a guardian?"

Gabriel shifted his gaze from the sliding glass doors to the young woman seated on the couch.

"I have heard you use both names and I wondered what the difference was."

Gabriel came and sat next to her on the couch.

"A Watcher is an angel who has been sent down to Earth to keep guard over the human race in general. A Guardian or Protector Angel has been assigned a specific human that they are to care for."

"Are you a guardian?" asked Roni.

"Oh no," said Gabriel. "I am a Watcher, and I also carry messages from the Creator to humans."

"Like Mary in the Bible?"

Gabriel smiled, "Yes. What a joy that assignment was! And what a sweet girl Mary was too. So young and willing to do whatever the Creator needed. She got a lot of ridicule from people for her obedience. Her father hit the roof when he found out she was pregnant. Her mother was embarrassed. Her family practically disowned her. And Joseph's heart was crushed too. Not a lot of men really loved their wives back then. Most marriages were arranged.

"Not Joseph, though. He loved Mary from the first moment he saw her. It nearly tore his heart out to think that she had been with another man. He was a tender soul. He was the right one to care for Mary and her Son. I was happy to be a messenger to him too. I never saw a man as relieved as he was."

"So what happens when a person dies? Does the angel quit being a guardian or what?"

"Well, there are different situations that an angel can come across. Like in your case, for example. Priscilla was your mother's guardian before you were born. When your mother died, she decided to stay on as your Protector. Some angels have a hard time disconnecting from their human when he or she dies. Angels get very emotionally attached to their charges. Sometimes they take another guardian assignment right away and sometimes they choose to be a Watcher for a while, until they are ready to take a protector position again.

"What about Michael? What is he?"

"Michael... Well, Michael is the Creator's right-hand angel, as you humans might say," said Gabriel, laughing a little with Roni. "Ralph and Uriel and I, we all have the title of Archangel like him, but he is the head guy. He has been in some pretty epic battles and he knows there is still an even greater battle to come. No one is as brave and self-sacrificing as he is. He is worthy of great respect."

Roni and Gabriel sat talking for a long time about angels and heaven and such. The rain continued to get heavier and heavier as the afternoon wore on. Around 3pm, the wind could be heard whistling through small gaps around the doors and windows of the old house. The bare trees outside began to bend in the wind. A branch from an old cottonwood tree broke and fell onto the patio just outside the glass doors of the family room. The noise startled Gabriel but Roni wasn't alarmed.

"It's just the Kansas wind whipping around. It's like this all the time here. Sometimes it sounds like we should go outside and expect to be in Oz, but we never are."

"Hmm. Something just does not feel quite right," Gabriel said as he looked out the doors once more. "I have had an uneasy feeling all day. I feel something stirring…"

"I have felt it too," said Uriel, walking into the room. "It is as though a dark presence has come with the storm."

"You guys haven't spent much time in Kansas, have you?" asked Roni. "These storms come and go all the time out here on the plains. We have a storm cellar out back if it gets too ugly."

She tried to lighten the mood with that last comment but, when she looked out at the black sky, she suddenly felt uneasy too.

"But then again, guys, we did have a town wiped off the map a few years back, so it never hurts to be cautious." As she finished her sentence, several small black dots could be seen off in the distance, moving in a path directly toward the house. Whatever they were, they were shrouded by the dark clouds that were now reaching down to the earth, like a child grasping for the last cookie at the bottom of the cookie jar.

A large bolt of lightning flashed across the sky. Its purple hue illuminated the wall of clouds and, for a moment, Roni thought she saw what looked like huge birds winging their way towards the house. A second bolt of lightning confirmed her previous observation; they were some sort of winged creatures.

"Roni," said Gabriel slowly. "You know that storm cellar you were just talking about?"

"Yes."

"You're going to need it. Take the children and their guardians and get down there as quickly as possible."

Then he looked at the other angel.

"Uriel, sound the alarm."

Both angels stepped out through the glass doors and once again shed their human appearances. Uriel put a large, golden ram's horn to his lips and blew a long, wave-like tone. The Watchers who stood guard around and above the house prepared themselves to do battle. Raphael joined Gabriel and Uriel at the glass doors.

***

Michael and Ryan were talking in the hallway of the hospital when Michael suddenly stopped speaking. He looked up and seemed to be listening to something.

"Ryan, I must go. The enemy has attacked," he announced.

The angel put his hand to his heart. "The sword of the Lord!" he shouted.

And then he was gone.

CHAPTER 21

The Nephilim

*"From birth I was cast upon you; from my
mother's womb you have been my God."*

Psalm 22:10, NIV

"Oriel!" Ryan called out.

"I am here," said the angel, who was standing right
behind him.

"Oriel, what's happening?" he grabbed the angel's
coat. "Where did Michael go? Who is the enemy
attacking? Is it Roni? Is she ok?"

"Do not fear, child. All will be well," Oriel tried to calm
Ryan down; but he could not.

"I have to get to her, Oriel," said Ryan frantically. "I
made a promise to her. I can't break it. I said I would
always be there for her and never leave her. I have to go
now. I won't let her down again."

"Michael and the others can handle the situation,"
began Oriel. "Just trust in…"

"I'm not leaving my responsibilities to someone else
again!" Ryan shouted at Oriel. "Now, are you coming with
me or not?"

The angel could see that he would not be able to
reason with the young man, so he relinquished his
position and told him to lead the way.

"Ok, I need my car." Ryan patted his pockets, trying
to find his keys. "It's back at the house. Where am I going
to get a car?"

"Does someone need a lift?" It was Madeline, who had
just walked out of a hospital room.

"Yes! Do you have a car I can use?" he asked bluntly. "Michael took off without me and it's an emergency."

"He does do that, doesn't he?" she smiled and tossed him her keys. "It's the green Honda out back. Just hit the unlock…"

But he was already gone.

***

"We've come for the girl," Ezekiel bellowed across the open field. "Give her to me and we will leave you in peace."

"More like pieces," said Ralph to Michael.

"You are right. He will not leave these humans in peace no matter what he gets," said Michael. "We must protect the girl at all costs. She could turn the battle for the human soul to the Dark One's favor if she is taken. The Creator wants to redeem her, though she has been conceived by this detestable creature."

"I created her. I gave her life. She belongs to me," Ezekiel echoed Michael's words, laying claim to the girl. But his deceitful ways were already know to the Creator and his angels.

"Only the Creator can give life, Ezekiel. You and your kind bring only death," Michael said to him. "This girl would not have the breath of life in her, had the Creator not ordained it. You know this can only end badly for you. Leave now and spare your armies another defeat."

His words angered Ezekiel.

"We will see who is defeated and who wins this battle! You have been warned!" he raised H'imesh-Dagon into the air. "For our master, the Shining One!"

Out of the mist emerged a troop of enormous figures. They looked like humans but were over twenty feet tall, with deep orange-colored wings that stretched out twice as far. They were dressed in black sarongs with blood-red belts. Their chests were bare, with a tattoo of a red dragon across them. Gold helmets with black plumes covered their heads, and a sword hung at each giant's side. The devilish creatures were holding spears, each weighing 100lbs, in their massive hands.

"The Nephilim have been reborn!" exclaimed Raphael, looking on in amazement at the line of half-human, half-angel abominations making their way to the house.

"Then it has begun," said Michael sadly.

Each side advanced until they were a mere fifty yards apart.

***

Up in Juli's bedroom, Roni and her sisters and Jillian were watching this parley between the two sides out in their backyard. Zoei looked up at Roni fearfully.

"What does he mean, you belong to him? You belong to us, Roni!" Zoei started to cry.

"It's ok, Zo Bear. Of course I belong to you and Jeni and Juli," Roni tried to comfort her sister. "That man is just trying to be mean."

"Let's go," she turned and led the way down the stairs. "Michael wants us all to go down and get in the storm cellar so we will be safe."

Juli followed Roni closely, but Jeni couldn't seem to tear herself away from the window. Jillian stood next to her but kept silent. Jeni was griping the window ledge with such force that it broke off in her hands. Roni knew she was getting worked up.

"Jeni, don't," said Roni. "Let the angels handle this. They know what they are doing. Come on, now!"

"Your sister is right, Jeni," Jillian chipped in. "You will accomplish nothing if you give our position away. It is obvious they want your sister. Remember what Michael said? We must protect her at all costs."

Juli walked over to Jeni and took hold of her arm. "Let's go, sergeant. Live to fight another day."

Jeni reluctantly went with her sister. Jillian and Raven took up a post outside, in front of the house. A terrific sound of clashing swords signaled that the battle had begun. Ariel, Priel, Samuel and Priscilla were already waiting for the sisters downstairs. The cellar was located to the right of the back porch, about fifteen feet out. The guardians had to get the children down inside, unseen by the enemy. They decided to crawl out through the dining room window at the side of the house, and then make their way to the cellar.

Priscilla went first. She crawled out the window and over to the cellar door. She lifted the handle gently and swung back one of the large doors. It hit the ground with a loud bang but no one could hear it over the sound of the raging battle. Juli and Ariel came out the window next. Juli leaned heavily on Ariel. She stumbled and almost fell down the cellar steps. Ariel scooped her up into her arms and carried her the rest of the way down. There were some old bunk beds at the back of the cellar. The angel laid her down on one to rest, as Juli had already lost consciousness.

Jeni and Samuel were about to leave when Roni grabbed her sister's arm. "Promise me that when you get out there, no matter what you see, you will get down in that cellar and stay hidden. No fighting. You hear me?"

Jeni rolled her eyes and promised reluctantly. She and Samuel made it round the corner of her house, but Jeni was not prepared for the fierceness of the battle going on outside. Her eyes grew wide with fright when she saw the giants and angels fighting, and she was somehow happy that Roni had made her promise not to fight. They made it down undetected. She went immediately over to Juli and took her by the hand and started to pray.

Priel dropped down outside the dining room window, and Roni handed Zoei through.

"Priel, guard my angel," she said.

"My life for hers," he assured her, disappearing around the corner of the house with the child.

Just as Zoei and Priel stepped away from the house, a head from a decapitated giant rolled right in front of them. Zoei let out a long shriek and buried her face in Priel's chest.

The secret was out. Several of the Nephilim had heard the scream, and their attention was drawn to the cellar. They started heading for the child and her guardian. Priscilla donned her angelic war apparel. She drew her sword and began to fight off the vicious attackers.

Roni, too, had heard her sister cry out. She jumped through the window and ran toward the cellar. She beheld a horrifying scene. The decapitated carcasses of giants were lying everywhere. Their heads lay in close proximity to their bodies. Priel and Zoei were trying to get to the cellar door, and Priscilla was struggling to protect them from an onslaught of attackers. Roni's heart was pounding in her chest. It felt as though it would burst. Her pacemaker vibrated wildly.

"Roni, get in the cellar!" Priscilla called out.

But Roni froze. Her feet wouldn't move. A Nephilim charged at her from the right. Priscilla managed to cut the creature's arm off, and blood splattered all over Roni. The giant rushed at her again, but Priscilla finished him off with one more thrust of her sword.

"Roni, get down in the cellar!" Priscilla pulled at the girl but she could not be moved.

A shiver went down Roni's spine and her hands began to tingle. "Oh no!" she cried. "Not this again!"

Two more of the winged creatures were making their way over to where Roni and Priscilla stood. Priscilla positioned herself right in front of Roni. Her sword was drawn and her footing sure.

"Priscilla!" screamed Roni. "Get away from me!"

"I'm not going to leave you!" the angel yelled back.

"Priscilla, move! I can't control it!"

Priscilla turned around and saw a blue light emanating from her charge's hands. Roni's eyes had begun to glow blue as well, and the angel knew what was about to happen. She grabbed the girl by the shoulders.

"You have to try and stop it, Roni. Come on, baby, I know you can do it!"

"I can't," cried Roni. "It's too powerful."

"Listen to my voice, sweet girl. Calm down. Can you hear me, Roni?"

"Yes, yes. I can hear you. I hear you, Priscilla."

"Come back to me, baby. Let your fear go." She took Roni's face in her hands. "Calm down, baby, calm down."

Roni's heart rate began to slow down as she concentrated on Priscilla's voice. The pounding in her ears lessened and her eyes were beginning to turn back to brown again.

Neither of them had their attention on the fight that was continuing around them. One of the Nephilim had secretly made his way around the back of the house. He crept up on the unsuspecting pair of women. He raised his sword and embedded it into the small of Priscilla's back. The connection she had with Roni was severed.

Priscilla cried out and fell to the ground like a lifeless doll. Roni screamed and knelt on the ground next to her guardian. Anger began to build up in her again as feelings of loss over Jason, her parents—and now Priscilla—rushed upon her all at once. It felt like an anvil had fallen on her chest. Her eyes began to glow blue again. Her hands started to tingle. The giant who had attacked her was fascinated by the sight of the glowing girl.

Roni turned around and looked at him. He looked down at the seemingly defenseless girl and raised his sword. Roni felt power rising in her. Without a thought, she stood up and threw a blue ball of light at the massive creature. It hit him in the chest and expanded across his whole body. He glowed blue for five seconds and then he was gone. He had disintegrated right before her eyes.

Roni couldn't believe what she had just seen. What she had just done. She sensed a familiar feeling rising within her. Pride. She had killed a giant. She alone had this power. She could defeat Ezekiel and his army of demons. She began to run with all her might, throwing blue balls of light at all the giants she could. They were disintegrating one by one. Her confidence was soaring.

Uriel was battling two of the giants by himself. His flaming swords were slicing the air like hot knives through butter. Roni took aim and killed both enemy soldiers at the same time. Uriel was shocked as the two Nephilim disappeared in front of him. He looked around for the source of the blue lightning. He saw Roni smiling at him. He wasn't sure how to respond to her, so he gave her a worried smile before continuing with the fight.

Michael saw Roni from across the field. He tried to get to her before she could cause any harm to herself or an angel. He pushed through the clamoring horde, taking down five more of the enemy.

"Roni, you must not use your powers yet, you don't know the extent of the damage you could do to yourself or others." He tried to warn her, but Roni was feeling invincible.

"I got this, Michael," she said as she took out two more giants. Nothing was going to stop her now. No longer was she the weak, overweight, nerdy cheerleader. She was taking on the Dark One and winning. On her own. No help from anyone. She felt awesome.

Just then she heard a familiar voice. The sound of Ezekiel's voice made her skin crawl.

"I knew you could do it, my child," he crowed. "Feel the power of your gifts. Use them to kill your enemies."

Roni turned around to face him. He looked delighted to see her in all her glory.

"You don't own me. You can't control me!" she shouted back in defiance. She summoned up all her power and threw a blue ball of light at him. He dodged the weapon easily.

"You think I don't know how to avoid your weapons? I created you," he bellowed. "I know everything about you. I am your father."

This last remark made Roni's blood boil. She could not contain her rage. She felt something strange going on in her body. It was more than just a tingling in her hands. Every part of her shivered and she started to feel lightheaded. She closed her eyes and tried to clear her mind.

When she opened her eyes again, she didn't recognize her surroundings. Her house looked far away and she was surrounded by fog. She thought the mist had rolled in up to the house.

"Ha, ha! You have surpassed my wildest expectations!" It was Ezekiel, but he sounded far away and below her.

She looked down at her feet and, to her surprise, she saw that she wasn't standing on the ground anymore. She was floating in the air. Ryan's fears had been realized in that moment. She shook her head to make sure she wasn't hallucinating. She wasn't. She was levitating at least fifty feet in the air.

From where she was, she could see her house and all the surrounding property. The dead bodies of the Nephilim littered the lawn. Angels and demons with swords, knives and axes were clashing below her and around her. She could see Jillian and Raven fighting off a few Nephilim at the front of the house. With her confidence boiling over, she began disposing of the dead bodies and disintegrating the enemy where they stood. One by one they ceased to exist. As she continued to eradicate the invaders, her energy level did not decrease. In fact, her strength and power increased with each exertion.

Ezekiel continued to observe his protégé as she killed one Nephilim after another. He was amused that she seemed to enjoy the obliteration of her adversaries. He let her continue until she had killed almost fifty of the giants.

"It's time to put a stop to her fun," he said to himself. He whispered some quick instructions to one of his soldiers. Then he positioned himself in front of Roni.

"Come, daughter of light. Let us leave this battlefield and go in search of new prey to eradicate."

"I am NOT your daughter!" Roni screamed at him.

She threw volley after volley of blue lightning at him, but he continued to elude her aim. This only further enraged her. She then focused all her energy on Ezekiel, trying to hit him with her weapon. But she could not.

So engrossed was she in trying to annihilate Ezekiel, she failed to notice the Nephilim creeping up on her. He knew exactly where to hit her. He took aim and drove his fist into the center of her back. She cried out in pain and fell to the ground.

She landed face down. It felt like every bone in her body was broken. She couldn't move, but she heard a familiar voice calling out to her.

"Oh baby. What have you done now?" It was Priscilla. She tried to get Roni to turn over but she couldn't move the girl.

"Come on, baby. Wake up," Priscilla patted Roni's cheek. "Wake up, sweetie."

"You're dead. I saw you die," Roni mumbled.

"You can't kill angels, baby. The Creator restored my strength so I could be with you."

"Finally I have you. I will make you the jewel in my crown." Ezekiel walked over to Roni.

"You will never have her!" Priscilla drew her sword and began to battle the huge angel. She was obviously outmatched in size and strength. Ezekiel kicked Priscilla across the field away from Roni. He stooped down to collect his prize. But before he could even touch her, he heard a shout coming from behind him.

"The sword of the Lord!"

It was Ryan.

CHAPTER 22

Jason

"We also rejoice in our sufferings, because we know that suffering produces perseverance; perseverance, character; and character, hope."

Romans 5:3-4, NIV

"Roni... Roni."

She could hear her name being called. She opened her eyes slowly. The light was so bright that she had to blink several times until her eyes adjusted to it. She was still lying on her stomach. Everything looked green. It was grass. She stroked it slowly between her fingers. A ladybug landed on a blade of grass right in front of her.

"Roni... Roni."

She heard her name again. The voice seemed familiar. She pushed herself up off the ground and looked around. She was surrounded by trees. The place seemed familiar. Like something from a dream... a dream so delightful you never want to wake up from it. She stood up. Her bare feet felt cool on the green grass.

Patches of clover were scattered throughout the small clearing. She leaned over and began to pick the tiny white flowers. The activity seemed familiar. A light breeze wisped her hair around her face. An old stump was to her left; she walked over and sat down. The spot seemed familiar. She began taking the clover flowers and tying them together to make a necklace. She hummed softly as she worked.

"Roni, where are you? I can't find you."

"I'm here, Jason, in our spot," she called out without even thinking.

Jason? Had she really heard his voice? She stood up and called to her long-lost friend again.

"Jason, I'm here. Waiting for you! Jason!"

From across the clearing, Roni saw the one person who could light up her day—Jason! She ran with all her might and jumped into his arms. They fell over and landed on the soft grass.

"Jason! Jason, I miss you."

She wouldn't let go of him. He started laughing.

"Roni! You have to let go of me so I can sit up," he said.

"Never," she cried. "I'm never gonna let you go."

He continued to laugh as he tried to sit up. Roni finally eased her hold on him. She sat back and looked at him.

Jason looked different. He looked healthy.

"What happened to you?" she asked.

"Heaven," he said and flexed his biceps. "It does a body good."

"Heaven? Is this heaven?" she asked. "Am I dead?"

Jason laughed, "Hardly. You're having a vision. You're dreaming."

"Well, if this is a dream, I never want to wake up!" she exclaimed.

Jason took her by the hand.

"Roni, you have to wake up. You have to help in the battle for the human soul."

"But I don't want to help. I want to stay here with you forever," she pleaded.

"This place isn't real anymore, Roni. It's only in your mind. Jeni and Juli and Zoei are real. You have to go back for them. You have to fight."

Roni jumped up and started pacing.

"I'm tired of fighting! I'm tired of being a mom. I'm tired of living with this machine in my chest! I just want to be a regular girl, not the savior of the world."

"You're hardly the Savior of the world, Roni," said Jason, laughing.

"You know what I mean. Why can't we just stay here in our special place? We had so many fun times here."

"I died here," said Jason solemnly.

Roni was quiet for a while. She laid her head down on Jason's lap and cried a little.

"When did you know that you were my brother?" Roni suddenly asked.

"I think I always knew, but I guess I was about ten when I said it out loud. I asked Oriel about it, and he explained what happened to me."

"Ya, and just when exactly were you going to tell me that you could see and talk to angels?" she sat up and punched him in the arm.

Jason smiled at her. "I figured you were going to be mad when you found out about that."

She rolled her eyes at him.

"Roni, seriously, the battle for life is going to go on whether you fight for it or not," Jason said gravely. "The decision, as to whether you are involved or not, has already been made for you. I'm sorry, you don't have a choice in that. When Ezekiel tampered with your conception, he thought he would have control over you. The Creator took that power from him and gave you a choice."

Jason took hold of her shoulders and looked her in the eyes. "You are special, Roni. You have talents and abilities that Ezekiel and his master want. They know you can extend the casualty list in this war. The Dark One knows that he will ultimately lose this war but—as to how many souls he takes with him—that is still undecided. You have the power to make that number higher or lower."

"I tried to use my powers for the Creator and I just landed flat on my face," she argued back.

"Were you really using your power for the Creator or was it for yourself?"

Roni turned and walked away from Jason. She knew that she had been caught in the sins of pride and selfishness again.

"I just don't want to be a nobody my whole life," she muttered.

"You aren't a nobody to the Creator," said Jason. "He knows each of his children by name. Each one is special. Look at these flowers. They are beautiful but they are just flowers. If the Creator takes time to make sure these flowers get food and water and sunshine so they can grow, don't you think he cares even just a little bit more about you? His own daughter."

"I am afraid to fight on my own, Jason. Ezekiel and his soldiers know exactly where my weak spot is."

"The Creator has made a promise to each of his children. He has promised that he will never leave you, and when you cry out he will send you aid."

She looked up at him sadly and said, "I miss you. When I go back, I won't see you anymore."

"You have to let me go, Roni. There are so many more friends for you to make. Please be comforted in the knowledge that I am in heaven and I am happy. Healthy too," he flexed his muscles again.

"And one more thing before you go back," he added. "Be good to Ryan. He loves you with a passion that can't be measured."

She smiled at Jason and blushed a little.

"Goodbye, Roni," he smiled back. "I love you and I'll see you—later."

She waved goodbye to her friend and brother.

CHAPTER 23

A Fight to the Finish

"I will lift up mine eyes unto the hills, from whence
cometh my help. My help cometh from the LORD,
which made heaven and earth."

Psalm 121:1-2

"Finally, I have you! I will make you the jewel in my crown."

"You will never have her! The sword of the Lord!"

Roni could just make out the figure of Ryan rushing toward her. He jumped and drove both of his feet into Ezekiel's chest. The evil angel was caught off guard and he stumbled back.

Ryan stopped and crouched over Roni's still body. He rolled her gently on her back and felt for a pulse on her neck. She was still alive.

"You have just made a grave mistake, human," Ezekiel growled as he picked himself up. "You will pay for that move. Draw your sword."

"My sword Eleazar is already drawn, you coward," said Ryan. "Stand up and face me."

Ezekiel charged at Ryan. He moved away from Roni to draw the angry demon away from her.

Roni could see Ryan out of the corner of her eye. He was crossing swords with Ezekiel. The fighting was fierce. It was still raining. Thunder rolled and lightning flashed. The angels continued to fight the demons but they were beginning to weaken as the battle wore on.

The Nephilim just kept coming; there seemed to be an endless stream of them. No matter how many were killed, more showed up to take their place. Uriel and several other angels had taken up positions around the cellar, where Jeni, Juli, Zoei and their protectors were hiding. If they were to fail in their struggle, Roni would be alone in the world. She felt helpless as she continued to lie motionless on the ground. She tried with all her might to move, but she couldn't. Trying to summon her powers again wasn't working. Every now and then, one of the giants would get near her, but Ryan came to her rescue again and again.

"What am I going to do?" she thought.

"You know." It was the voice again.

"I know what?" Roni asked.

"You know what to do when you're in trouble."

"I do?"

"Yes."

 I've never been in a good angel *vs* bad angel battle before this, so I'm kind of new to this scenario."

"Why do you fight against me, my darling?"

I'm not fighting, I'm... um... just trying to... ah... be self-sufficient. I take care of my sisters, I run the house and pay the bills, I made it to captain of my cheer squad. Surely I can get my powers to kick back in, so I can help win this war."

"I am here to help you, if you would only call on me."

"I want to do this myself!" she exclaimed.

"Then you will fail."

Tears filled Roni's eyes. She knew what she needed to do, but why was it so hard? Giving up control of her life to someone else, a higher power, seemed like it should be an easy thing to do. But it wasn't. Ever since Jason died, she had tried to control everything in her life, in the hope that something bad like that would never happen again. Then her father had died and, after that, her mother. It seemed like her life was spinning out of control.

Now, here she was, lying flat on her back. She had this amazing power and she couldn't even get it to work right. All this power, and she was as weak and as vulnerable as a baby. She remembered something her mother had once said to her: *Sometimes God has to knock you flat on your back to get you to look up.* Well, she was flat on her back and looking up now.

A loud crash to her right distracted her. She was able to turn her head slightly. Ryan and Ezekiel were still in a heated battle, and Ezekiel was beginning to get the upper hand. They moved out of Roni's line of sight and she was able to see the horizon beyond. A small rise in the plain caught her attention, mostly because eighty percent of Kansas is flat. This small hill seemed to be hiding a ray of sunshine. She thought of the passage she had read earlier that day.

"I will lift up mine eyes unto the hills, from whence cometh my help. My help cometh from the LORD, which made heaven and earth."

She began to say the verses out loud.

"He will not suffer thy foot to be moved: he that keepeth thee will not slumber."

Something was happening! It looked like the sun had begun to rise.

"Behold, he that keepeth Israel shall neither slumber nor sleep." Roni felt the strength returning to her body.

"The LORD is thy keeper," she shouted joyfully. It was becoming brighter and brighter all around her.

"The LORD is thy shade upon thy right hand," she sat up and proclaimed. "The sun shall not smite thee by day, nor the moon by night."

As it got lighter, a cry went up from the Nephilim.

"The LORD shall preserve thee from all evil: he shall preserve thy soul." Roni stood up.

"The LORD shall preserve thy going out and thy coming in from this time forth, and even for evermore!" Roni stood up to her full height and hit her heart with her fist.

"The sword of the Lord," she shouted. Immediately her earthly apparel was shed and she stood there in the armor of the Creator, a sword aflame in her hand.

The cry of the Nephilim was increasing, and Roni could see why. As the clouds began to roll back, the light of the sun was burning their skin and they were disintegrating. Their numbers were diminishing before Ezekiel's eyes.

"Ahhhh," he cried, seeing the last remnants of his army disappear.

As the angels began to cheer, Ryan looked across the lawn and saw Roni dressed in her battle gear. He smiled and was about to walk over to her when he felt an immense pressure on his chest. Like someone was squeezing his ribcage. He stood still for a moment, then fell backwards to the ground. Ezekiel had slammed his sword across Ryan's chest.

"Nooooooo!" Roni screamed.

She ran and leapt at Ezekiel. He jumped towards her as well. Her flaming sword hit his with a deafening blow. She felled blow after blow on him. He struck back.

The angels wanted to help her, but Michael held them back. "Roni must stand on her own faith in the Creator," he said.

Ezekiel landed a blow on Roni's chest, and she was knocked back to where Michael and the others were standing.

"You must not turn your back on him," said Michael as he helped her up. "You have no armor to protect you there." Roni nodded in acknowledgment.

Gabriel was holding Priscilla's hand. The girls and their protectors came up out of the cellar. They saw their sister brawling with this enormous angel.

"Roni!" screamed Jeni. She tried to run to her sister's help but Samuel held her back.

"Michael has commanded us to let her finish this on her own," he said.

"You can, however, strengthen her," Michael said to them from behind.

The girls turned around. He looked at them tenderly. Jeni and Juli were confused.

Michael looked at Zoei.

"I will leave this to you, little one."

Then he walked away, saying to himself, "And a little child shall lead them."

"Why are we leaving our sister's fate to a five-year-old?" asked Jeni.

"Jeni," said Juli, placing her hand on the shaking girl, "Zoei knows what to do. We all know what to do. Take my hand."

The girls joined hands and Zoei began to pray, "Abba, please help Roni to be strong. Don't let the bad Mr Ezekiel hurt her. Please protect her. Amen."

Zoei faced the battlefield and began to shout, "Deliver me from mine enemies, O my God: defend me from them that rise up against me. (*Psalm 59:1*)"

Jeni and Juli looked down at their little sister in awe.

"Preserve me, O God: for in thee do I put my trust! (*Psalm 16:1*)" she yelled out again. The crystal on her necklace began to glow white.

Priel elbowed Uriel. "That's my girl," he said.

Roni could feel her body strengthening. She landed several blows on Ezekiel's arm, then kicked him in his side. He fell into the side of the house, making a large, gaping hole in the family room. Roni looked over to her sisters and grinned. She readied herself for Ezekiel's next attack.

He came at her fast, jumped over her and landed behind her. She whipped around quickly, remembering where her kill switch was. He lunged at her and jabbed his sword at her throat. She stepped back and dodged his intended blow. He grew infuriated at her resilience.

Jeni decided it was her turn to speak. "The LORD is my light and my salvation; whom shall I fear?"

Then Juli added, "The LORD is the strength of my life; of whom shall I be afraid? (*Psalm 27:1*)"

The twins reached out their hands to each other and to their littlest sister. Then, all three holding hands together, they shouted, "Keep me, O LORD, from the hands of the wicked; preserve me from the violent man. (*Psalm 140:4a*)" All their necklaces were glowing brightly. "The LORD is my rock, and my fortress, and my deliverer; my God, my strength, in whom I will trust; my buckler, and the horn of my salvation, and my high tower. (*Psalm 18:2*)"

Ryan was regaining consciousness. He could hear a fight going on around him but he couldn't see it. Although he could barely breathe, he began to call upon the Creator, "LORD, I cry unto thee: make haste unto me; give ear unto my voice, when I cry unto thee. (*Psalm 141:1*)" Roni's necklace, which he was wearing, began to glow. He looked at it curiously.

Another hard kick from Roni, and Ezekiel landed within ten feet of Ryan. He saw the crystal glowing on Ryan's neck and began crawling toward the human. Reaching out, he snatched the necklace from around Ryan's neck. He wailed in pain as the glowing crystal burned through his hand. Ezekiel lay on his back next to Ryan, writhing in pain. Out of the corner of his eye, he could see Roni running toward him. He lifted his elbow and crashed it down on Ryan's chest.

Ryan looked up at Roni. Then his heart stopped.

CHAPTER 24

Saving Ryan

*"Greater love hath no man than this, that
a man lay down his life for his friends."*

John 15:13

"In the name of the Lord!" Roni shouted.

She jumped and aimed for Ezekiel. As she came down out of the air, she wrapped both hands around the hilt of her sword and plunged it into the fallen angel's heart. The strike caught him by surprise. The flesh on his body burned away, and he let out a howl of defeat.

"I know things," he sneered. "Things about your mother's death. Things..."

"Flee, you evildoer," Michael commanded. "Oppress these children no more!"

Ezekiel hissed at Michael and evaporated into the air.

"Michael, Michael! He knows something about my mother!" Roni cried as she fell to her knees. "You should have let him finish!"

She was exhausted and Michael knew this. He knelt down and held her closely as she cried.

"The enemy will always try to bargain when his back is against the wall," he said. "Never give up the high ground when they have nothing to lose and you have everything to lose." Though the angel was feeling weak himself, he tried to pass some of his strength to her.

As Roni revived, she remembered Ryan. "Ryan! Ryan!" she laid her head on his chest. She could not feel a heartbeat. "No, no!" she wailed. "No! You can't die!"

She put her hands on his chest and started CPR. She pumped his heart for over ten minutes, but she still couldn't get a rhythm. She beat her fists on his chest, then she pumped his heart some more. She blew her own breath into his lungs. Nothing worked.

"Roni, it's over," Priscilla knelt down next to the girl and stroked her hair. "Ryan's purpose on the earth must be over or the Creator would not have taken him."

Roni just couldn't accept that another person she loved was dead. She started hitting his chest again. She turned her eyes heavenward and cried out, "Help me, God! Help me! Show me what to do!"

"You know what to do."

Roni got quiet. "I do?" she asked.

"You do."

And suddenly she did know. She bowed her head and closed her eyes. "My Father in heaven, please grant me the ability to use my power to heal this man. Amen."

With her eyes still closed, she put her hands together over Ryan's chest. The blue light began to glow between her fingers. Her eyes glowed once again as she prepared to use her power. She tore his t-shirt open and placed her hands on his bare torso. She placed one hand under his left arm, near the bottom of his rib cage, and the other on his chest.

She wasn't quite sure how to regulate the amount of energy she was about to put through his body. After a minute or two, she decided to trust the Creator to manage the flow of electricity so it would not fry him. She proceeded to focus her full power on Ryan's heart.

Suddenly she felt a sharp pain through the palms of her hands. Ryan's body jumped. She looked at the burn marks on her hands and then to Ryan. He had not begun to breathe. Again she placed her hands on his body and focused another volt of energy through him. The pain in her hands was so excruciating that she cried out. The burn marks were bleeding, but Ryan was still dead. A third time she shocked him, and still no response. A fourth and fifth time caused her body to revolt against her. The burn marks were now black and had burned through to the back of her palms. She cried out in agony.

"Creator, please help me endure!" Once more she put her hands on Ryan. The pain was so excruciating that she nearly blacked out. Priscilla tried to get her to stop, but Roni was relentless.

"He would not give up on me. I will not give up on him!" she cried.

One last time she placed her hands on him and let out a cry, "In the name of the Lord!"

She released the energy and her body went limp. She collapsed on top of Ryan's body.

***

Roni was trying to sleep when she felt something moving under her. She wriggled a bit to try to get comfortable, but the movement wouldn't stop. She opened her eyes and suddenly remembered where she was.

"Ryan!"

She sat up. She could see that his stomach was rising and falling. She put her ear to his chest. His heart was beating.

"Ryan. Ryan, wake up."

Ryan opened his eyes slowly. He blinked rapidly until he could adjust to the light. When he could finally see clearly, the most beautiful face he had ever known was looking down at him. Roni.

He smiled at her, then reached up and touched her face. "I saved you," he said softly.

She smiled and leaned over and put her forehead on his.

"I saved you back."

CHAPTER 25

The Man in the Picture

"For since the creation of the world God's invisible qualities—his eternal power and divine nature—have been clearly seen, being understood from what has been made, so that men are without excuse."

Romans 1:20, NIV

Sunday 10ᵗʰ November

China lay on the table as the x-ray tech lined up the machine to get a picture of her chest. She had never had an x-ray before, so this was a new experience for her. A very cold experience, that was for sure. She could hardly feel her toes anymore. She looked over to the window, where the technician was checking the computers to make sure her pictures weren't blurry.

Neil was standing near the window, watching her. It made her feel a little self-conscious to have someone's eyes on her all the time but he didn't look at her like he wanted something, so her anxiety lessened.

"Who is he and where did he come from?" she wondered. She thought back to yesterday, when she had cried out for help, and he and Anastasia had appeared out of nowhere. At the time, she was too exhausted to question their sudden appearance, but she did remember them saying that they came from heaven.

She knew a little about heaven from the old lady who had taken care of her in Russia. She had given her a book with pictures of heaven and angels. Her nurse had told her that God lived in heaven with his angels. It was beautiful there. Trees and flowers and soft green grass were everywhere. You could pick fruit off any tree and eat it. The streets were made of pure gold and the gates around heaven were giant pearls. There were lots of animals that you could pet and play with, and they were all nice, even the bears and lions. Everyone had a big house to live in. Nobody was sad there, and nobody would hurt you.

The most important thing that you did in heaven was sing to God and thank him for making such a wonderful place for his children to go when they die. Anastasia said that Trinity was there and that she was with her Father; but she didn't have a Father. China thought that Anastasia must have been confused. China and Trinity had never talked about God or angels or anything like that. She wondered if her friend had ever even heard about God.

Sometimes at night, after she had been with Joseph or one of his customers, she would lie in bed and cry. At such times, she would feel like someone was there, in her room. Someone would be with her. She couldn't see him, but she knew he was there and she felt safe again. That was how she felt when she was with Neil.

The whole x-ray process took about an hour. Ryan had wanted her x-rayed from head to toe. When it was over, Neil came and picked her up. He sat her gently in her wheelchair and knelt before her.

"I have a little present for you," he said.

It had been a long time since she had received a gift from anybody who didn't want something in return. She frowned a little, but her guardian touched her hand softly and she felt peaceful again. He presented her with a pair of pink slippers.

"I saw that you kept rubbing your feet together, so I figured you might be cold." He lifted her cold feet one at a time and put the slippers on her. They were soft inside, like her kitten's fur. She wiggled her toes around in them. "They have a hard sole, so you can even walk outside in them."

"Thank you," China said quietly.

"Are you hungry? I could take you over to the cafeteria to get some lunch."

"Can you take me to my baby first? I haven't seen her all morning."

Neil smiled and pointed her chair toward the hospital nursery. As they made their way down the hall, China noticed the pictures on the wall. They were of a man dressed in a robe. He had long brown hair and a full beard. In each picture, he was touching people who looked like they were sick or disabled in some way. They came to a very large picture of the man, and he had a lot of children around him.

"Stop!" China cried out.

She startled Neil, and he rushed around to the front of the chair to see what she needed. She looked beyond Neil's head at the face of the man in the picture. He seemed familiar. She put her hand on Neil's shoulder and pulled herself up on her feet.

When she reached the picture, she examined the man closely. She touched his face, trying to make herself remember where she had seen him before.

"It is a fairly good likeness," Neil said.

"You know this person?"

"Yes, of course. He is Jesus. The Creator's Son."

"The Creator?"

"The Creator is the designer of all things. He made the universe and everything in it."

"Oh." She had never thought about where everything came from before. All her life she had just been trying to survive what was going on around her.

"I know this man from somewhere, but I can't remember where. He wasn't a customer or a doctor at the facility. Maybe I saw him in a dream or something."

"He does tend to show up in the most unusual places," said Neil, laughing a little.

She couldn't take her eyes off the picture for a long time. He wasn't the most handsome man she had ever seen, but there was something about his face that made her feel almost joyful inside. She motioned to Neil that she was ready to go back to her chair. She was determined to remember where she had seen this man's face, so she tucked the memory of him away in her mind.

When they arrived at the nursery, it seemed like every infant there was crying. China looked around for her baby. She stood up and saw her in the back row. She had a little pink bonnet on, and she was looking up at the ceiling and cooing.

"She sees her guardian," said Neil.

China looked around for Anastasia but she couldn't find her. "Where?"

"Look over by the baby again." Neil put his hand on her shoulder and, when she turned her head back over to her baby, she could see the shimmering outline of the angel leaning over the crib and speaking to the infant.

She blinked her eyes several times to make sure she wasn't hallucinating. When she looked around the room again, she could see an angel beside every cradle that had a baby in it. Even the nurses and doctors each had a shining angel following them.

"Wow," China said. "What is going on? What am I seeing?"

"The Creator has opened your spiritual eyes so that you might see what is happening in the spirit world."

China sat there in awe at what she was seeing. Could there be more to this world than what she had seen so far in her life? Something beyond the slavery of her recent past? Suddenly down the hall she heard a door slam. She turned to where the noise had come from and saw a horrifying sight.

An angel with a red dragon on his chest came storming down the hall after a tall, overweight man. His stomach hung over his belt as if he had drunk nothing but beer his whole life. He looked like he needed a shave and he reeked of cigarette smoke. He was mumbling and cursing as he passed China and her guardian. Neil put his arms around her, covering her whole body with his wings. The evil angel sneered at them as he passed. Neil looked with pity on the man. China buried her face in Neil's chest until the pair were out of sight. She was trembling from head to toe.

"Do not fear, my child. I will never leave you. You are safe."

"Wh...what was that?" China was barely able to get the words out.

"That was a man who has rejected the Creator. He has chosen to do evil instead of good. He would not let his guardian help him, so an enemy angel has taken up residence with him."

"He reminded me of Joseph," said China.

"Joseph can't harm you anymore. He has his reward."

***

The nurses made China wash her hands and put on a yellow gown before she could hold the baby. As she held the tiny bundle in her arms, China felt a great wave of love sweeping over her. The baby was so beautiful. Her lips were full and red and perfect. Her bottom lip stuck out slightly, giving her a pouty look. Her skin was soft and white, except for her cheeks, which were a creamy rose color. China reached up and pulled the little bonnet off the baby's head, and out tumbled a mass of dark brown curls. Tears welled up in the girl's eyes.

"She looks just like Trinity," she said, holding the baby close to her.

"What a lovely child! Does she have a name yet?" asked Neil.

"No. She was supposed to be sold. Trinity and I couldn't bring ourselves to name her."

Just then the baby stretched and yawned. She opened her eyes and blinked her long dark lashes. She looked around for a few seconds, her blue eyes as round as saucers. Then she closed her eyes again. Her lips made a perfect O shape as she arched her back and continued to stretch. Neil smiled and asked if he could hold her.

"Every child is such a miracle," he said as he looked down at the little sleeping beauty in his arms.

The nurse came and gave China a bottle for the baby. When she had had enough to drink, Neil showed the young woman how to put the child over her shoulder and burp her. China held her for another twenty minutes until the nurse came to take her back to her crib. She was sad to part with her sweet little angel.

"Let's see," said the nurse. "Baby Miller, right? You'd better come up with a name for this sweetie pie or she's going to be confused with all the nicknames the staff have given her."

The cheerful nurse walked away with the baby, leaving China to wonder why she had called the child Baby Miller. She looked down at her hospital ID bracelet. It said China Miller. It was strange to be so quickly adopted by this doctor. Maybe he really was her brother and he would take care of her, like he said. She could always hope.

***

After lunch, Neil took China back to her room and tucked her into her bed. She was just about to ask the angel about her mother when she heard a knock at her door. It was Ryan.

"Hi, how's my favorite sister?"

China looked blankly at Ryan, wondering what he was talking about. Then she realized he was referring to her. "Oh... uh... you mean me. Sorry, I'm not used to... um... being related to... um... anybody."

He smiled at her. "Well, you'd better get used to it because I'm not going away anytime soon. How are you feeling?"

"I'm ok, I guess, just a little sore. My neck is itchy."

"That would be the healing process. I'm afraid I can't do anything about it. Just don't scratch it. I'm hoping we can keep it from scarring too much."

China laughed sarcastically. "Why? It will just go with all the other ones on my body."

Ryan didn't laugh. In fact, he got a little teary-eyed. He pulled out her x-rays and went over them with her. It looked like she had broken three ribs and two of her fingers in the last five years. She had compression fractures on two of her vertebrae and an old skull fracture that hadn't healed completely. He could tell that her nose had been broken at least once. Her collar bones had been cracked when she was younger but she couldn't remember ever being hurt there.

Her body was covered in various-sized scars, including a large, three-inch one on her upper left arm. It looked like it had gone down very deep into her skin. She told Ryan that one of Joseph's customers had punched her there, and he had a ring on his finger that hooked onto her skin and tore it open when she tried to pull away from him. She had numerous other small injuries that she and Ryan talked about. She was so matter-of-fact about them that he felt like walking down to the jail and inflicting the same injuries on her former master. Hopefully, she would never have to worry about him again.

She was a little anemic and was in need of plenty of sunshine. "Sunshine has a multitude of benefits," he told her, "including helping with depression. The nurses are going to give you several vitamin and protein shakes to help build up your immune system. I've also prescribed some vitamin B shots for..." he stopped, for she was looking up at him as though he were speaking a foreign language. "What is it, China?"

She looked away from him. Her cheeks were turning red. A single tear slid down her face, but she wiped it away quickly and tried to sound like she wasn't embarrassed. "I have absolutely no idea what you just said," she whispered.

Now it was Ryan's turn to feel embarrassed. He had not taken into account the fact that this girl had been locked up all her life and probably never heard of vitamins and immune systems and such.

"I'm sorry, I don't know what to say to make you understand. I guess you'll just have to trust me."

Oops... that was even better. Now he was asking this frail little bird to put her trust in a complete stranger—and a man at that. He felt like an insensitive idiot.

China could tell that he was nervous. She tried to put him at ease. "I can read," she said meekly. "Perhaps, if you have a book about... well, whatever you were just talking about, I might be able to understand stuff... more... um... better."

"That's a great idea! What about an iPad? Then you could look up things on the internet and..."

She was looking confused again.

"Never mind. I will bring you a book. Maybe later you can learn about computers."

He took to writing some things on her chart for a few minutes. If he was writing, maybe he could stop putting his foot in his mouth every other sentence. When he had finished, China spoke up. She wanted to know why the nurses had called the child Baby Miller.

"Well, everyone needs a last name, you and the baby as well. I thought it might make you feel like you two belong in my family. I'm sorry if I was too hasty in giving it to you."

"No, it's fine. I was just surprised. I've only ever been just China my whole life."

"I see. I have a few questions for you, if you don't mind answering them," said Ryan.

"That's fine," she replied.

"Ok, well, do you remember where you were born? What town in Russia?"

"I don't," China answered. "I was inside the facility most of the time."

"What about landmarks and things like that? What did it look like when you were outside?"

"When I did get to go outside, the ground was black—kind of like charcoal—and there were lots of trees that had fallen down."

"Must have been near Norilsk. Was the facility in a town or out in the wilderness?"

"I remember being able to see the tops of some buildings over the trees, when I went outside. I know that, before we could reach the exit door, we had to walk through a very long tunnel. Maybe the facility was in town, but a tunnel was made so that the doctors and staff could leave secretly."

"That sounds plausible. I have a friend over there who might be able to tell us if a secret entrance still exists. I took pictures of the town when I was there a few months ago. If you want to, we could look at them sometime and see if you remember anything else."

"That sounds like it would be fun." For the first time, China smiled a genuine smile at Ryan. He was happy to see it.

"Dr Parker said she would come by and see you this afternoon. I told her about you and she thinks she can fix your lip quite easily."

China stopped smiling and looked down at her hands again.

"That would be great."

"Ryan, you're an idiot!" he said to himself.

"I have to go and check on my other patients. I'll come and see you later." He patted his sister and took himself off before he could commit another gaffe.

CHAPTER 26

Rest after Battle

*"Come to me, all you who are weary and burdened,
and I will give you rest."*
Matthew 11:28, NIV

After the rescue at Joseph's place, everyone except Ryan and his patients had gone straight back to the lake house. Upon their arrival there, they had been surprised to see that a great battle had just been fought around the house, with Roni and Ryan at the center of it all. It was a good thing it was late fall or there would have been other people around the lake, and the questions could have been interesting.

Jared and Jillian had volunteered to help drive the sisters and Ryan to the hospital in Wichita. It was obvious that Roni and Ryan needed medical attention, and Jillian had a few cuts and bruises of her own.

"Nothing stitch-worthy," Jillian had declared; but she would go to the hospital to appease her guardian. She had Roni, Ryan and Zoei in her car.

Jared drove the other car and Jeni sat up front with him. Anyone could see she was enjoying every minute of his attention. Juli slept all the way in the back seat.

***

"Back in the hospital again. And I just got out of this place a week ago," Roni muttered as she looked at the bandages on her hands.

Saving Ryan had taken its toll on her body. He had tried to heal her hands again but without success. She figured that the Creator wanted her to think long and hard before she used her powers. She wasn't feeling the repercussions of being hit in the back as badly as the last time it had happened. She was sure she had the Creator to thank for that.

Juli was in the bed next to her. She hadn't been the same since she was attacked by the rogue angel. Roni could hear the sound of her heart monitor. It was beeping very slowly, so she thought her sister must be asleep. Ariel was standing guard next to her bed. Roni would never forget the sight of this petite angel wielding a battle axe against her foes.

Her thoughts wandered back to the battle she had just fought and won. She thought about how she was able to put on her spiritual armor and fight for her family. She gave thanks in her heart to the Creator for his mercy and kindness.

Just then Ryan walked into her room.

"How's it going, Rapunzel?"

Roni rolled her eyes at him on hearing the nickname. "There's no use fighting it," she thought. "Good. How about you? How are your ribs feeling? Shouldn't you be resting?"

"Some of us have patients to attend to," said Ryan. "We can't afford to lounge around in hospital beds just because we have two broken ribs. Besides, I'm taped up good and taking pain medication, so I should be fine. I'm a fast healer."

Ryan sat on the side of her bed.

"I can't believe how quickly you have recovered," said Roni. "I wonder if your healing powers have anything to do with it."

"It must. I was just checking on China. Her wounds are healing quickly as well. It was pretty awesome when she began to revive the baby with me."

"How is your sister doing?" asked Roni.

"Good, I think. I just keep saying stupid things around her. She must think I'm an imbecile."

Roni laughed. "Why don't you just be yourself? I think you're overthinking things. You do get a little stupid when you overcompensate."

"I just want her to feel like she has a family she can turn to if she needs something."

"It will probably be a long time before she realizes that you are sincere. In fact, she may never be able to fully accept your love. Remember, she has had eighteen years to build up emotional walls. Those won't come down just because you saved her."

"Where did you get all your counseling smarts? You seem to have all the answers on emotional healing."

As soon as the words were out of his mouth, Ryan knew that he had stepped in it again.

"Sorry, Roni, that was a dumb question. I was very sad to hear that your parents had died."

"Ya... um... I don't really want to talk about that right now. Tell me how you and Jeni are coming on, figuring out what's up with me. I don't know if you've heard, but I can fly."

"I did hear that. I'm not really surprised. We did figure out that you should be able to do almost anything that has to do with magnetism or electricity, but apparently not without a price," he said as he pointed to her hands.

"Great, now you tell me. Do you think Jason had the same nanites in his blood?"

"I don't think so, or they would have been seen in his blood tests. When your heart gave out, I defibrillated you several times before I could get a pulse, but I don't know why your heart could not sustain you before I shocked you."

"Didn't your parents take Jason to the doctor a lot? Perhaps studying his medical records will provide you with some answers."

"I took Jason's records with me the day I left for Germany. I even got an autopsy faxed to me after his funeral. They didn't give me much information except what I already figured had happened. He had a blood clot that went to his already weak heart."

Both of them were out of hypotheses to explain what had happened. It was quiet for a few minutes, then Roni spoke again. "I never thanked you for saving my life again yesterday."

"You know I would do anything for you, Roni," Ryan said as he took her hand.

Roni looked at Ryan and knew he was sincere. She just wasn't sure if she was able to go all in yet. She needed time. They had been thrown together only a few weeks ago, and too much was happening for her to decide on a relationship just yet.

They were interrupted by a knock on the door. Jeni, Zoei and Jared came into the room. Jared was still following Jeni everywhere she went. He didn't want to leave her side, now that they had met up again.

"Roni, you're not going to be in the hospital forever again, are you?" asked Zoei.

"Not this time, Zo Bear; in fact, as soon as Dr Miller says so, I get to go home."

Zoei looked at Ryan. She clasped her hands together and batted her eyelashes at him, like she was begging for more TV time or dessert.

"It would be fabulous of you, Dr Miller, if you let my sister come home," she pleaded as sweetly and persuasively as she could.

"Now, how can you resist that?" said Jeni, and everyone laughed.

"Ok, ok. I know when I'm beaten. As soon as I make sure your sister's burns are on their way to getting better, I will let her out of hospital prison."

Zoei was satisfied with that answer.

***

About 5pm, all Roni's blood tests and x-rays were finished, and she was ready to leave the hospital. The only problem was the huge hole in the living room that Ezekiel had made. Roni suggested that they stay in a hotel in Wichita that night. That way they could be close to the hospital when China and the children were released the next day. Everyone agreed to this temporary arrangement, except Jeni and Jared.

Jeni was not about to leave Juli alone again—and Jared, well, he wasn't going to leave Jeni alone. So, the two of them stayed in the hospital room with Juli. Jeni slept on the bed that had been Roni's and Jared slept in the chair. The guardians kept watch.

***

It felt so good to be in a decent bed again. Hospital beds could be so hard on a person's back. Roni was happy that they had found a motel room with two queen-size beds.

She and Zoei were in one bed and Jillian was in the other. The white walls and the brown-and-orange striped curtains in the room were nothing to write home about, but once the lights were out they wouldn't matter. As long as no bugs were crawling on them, the girls couldn't care less what the room looked like.

Besides her hands, her back was hurting too, right where the Nephilim had hit her. She wondered what the bruise looked like now. Had Ezekiel designed this kill switch, as she called it, in case she decided she didn't want to be on his team? The team trying to wipe out humanity. He must have known there was a possibility that might happen.

She tried to imagine what happened back when she and Ryan and Jason were just babies. How could Oriel be Jason and Ryan's guardian? That didn't make sense. It seems like each of us has a guardian of our own, even if we are twins. She figured that would be a question for Priscilla in the morning. Right now, all she wanted was to sleep for a very long time...

CHAPTER 27

Allyson Trinity Miller

*"Peace I leave with you, my peace I give unto you:
not as the world giveth, give I unto you. Let not
your heart be troubled, neither let it be afraid."*

John 14:27

Monday 11th November

Roni could feel someone staring at her as she slept. She opened one eye, and there was Zoei looking at her.

"Time to get up! No sleeping past ten!" Zoei sang out.

Roni reached for her phone to check the time.

"It's only 6am, Zo! It's not time for me to be conscious, let alone be up out of bed. Watch the Disney channel or something."

Roni buried her head in her pillow and tried to block out the sound of the TV. It wasn't working. The music on TV was telling Zoei to dance, so the little girl decided to do her own choreography. She jumped from bed to bed, back and forth, back and forth, for ten straight minutes. Roni wondered why Jillian wasn't yelling at Zoei for disturbing her sleep. Finally she sat up and saw that the other bed was empty. She could hear the shower running.

"Nice. Another morning person," she mumbled.

Jillian came out of the bathroom a few minutes later, wrapped up in a towel. She had another towel on her head that looked like a turban.

"She still looks like she should be on the cover of a magazine, even when she's only wearing towels," thought Roni. "Great. I probably look like I've slept in a wind tunnel all night."

All three girls were ready to check out of their motel room by eight o'clock. None of them had packed a bag, so they just put the clothes they had on from the day before. Jillian, of course, had the full line of travel-size Mary Kay makeup products with her, so she looked like a million bucks. Roni looked in the mirror and thought she looked like 25 cents.

***

Back at the hospital, Juli was doing a lot better. She had slept peacefully all night, so she was well rested. Jared went down to the cafeteria and got her something to eat, since she had slept through the hospital's regular breakfast time. Eggs, bacon and grits were her favorite, and she ate every bit that was on her plate.

After seeing that Juli was doing much better, Roni thought she would go and meet Ryan's sister. She was a little nervous. She was expecting another Barbie-doll girl like Jillian, but instead she found a skinny, blond-haired girl with big blue eyes and ghostly white skin. She had a black eye and a large bandage on her neck. Her nails were brittle and peeling, and her hair was in desperate need of a cut and conditioning treatment. Looking at her made Roni feel thankful that she had ended up in her adoptive parents' home and not in a nightmare, like this pathetic-looking creature lying in a hospital bed.

"Hi. I'm Roni. I'm a friend of your brother Ryan." She held out her hand to the pale girl. China's fingers were like ice. "Are you cold? I could have one of the nurses bring you a heated blanket."

China smiled at this beautiful person in front of her. She couldn't take her eyes off Roni's face.

190

"Are you an angel too?" she asked.

Roni laughed. "I don't think so. I don't have enough patience to be one."

"My nurse gave me a book once. It had a lot of pictures in it. You look like one of the angels."

"Well, I am flattered," said Roni, not really knowing how to respond to such a nice compliment. "How are you feeling?"

China wasn't sure how to answer the question. Physically she felt like she had been dragged 100 yards behind a truck, and emotionally... well... like she had been dragged 1000 yards behind a truck. So all she said was "fine".

Roni looked at China's face and noticed a small, whitish spot on her cheek, just like the one Ezekiel had given her. She reached out her hand to touch China's face and the girl backed away.

"Oh, I'm so sorry. I just saw the spot on your face and I... well, I have one too."

She brushed her hair back, so the girl in the bed could see the white mark on her face. China reached out her hand and Roni allowed her to touch her face. She concentrated on the spot for a moment, as if she could wipe it away; but it could not be done.

"Ezekiel," said Roni softly.

China just nodded her head.

Roni decided that it would be best to change the subject. She wasn't a great conversationalist herself, so talking with China was kind of like talking to herself. She decided to ask her about things she herself found interesting.

"What kind of movies do you like?" Roni asked.

"I haven't seen one for a very, very long time. Not since I was in the facility in Russia. I liked them when I was little, so I figure I will still like them now."

Roni thought she could detect a slight accent when China spoke. It was pretty.

"Well, let's go catch a movie when you're feeling better."

China began to feel more relaxed as Roni kept talking to her. It was nice to have someone wanting to know what she liked. Within half an hour they were talking and laughing like they were old school friends. Ryan walked up to the door at one point. He could hear the two girls chatting happily together, so he decided not to spoil their fun. He would come back to check on China later.

A nurse brought the baby in. Roni was delighted to see the tiny mite. She remembered how excited she had been when her mom and dad brought Zoei home.

"If you want to take this baby home any time soon, you had better come up with a name for her, or it's going to say Sweet Heart Miller on her birth certificate," the nurse cautioned.

The girls laughed. "I'll make sure this cutie pie has a name by the time you come back to get her," Roni said to the nurse as she picked the baby up.

"Good luck," the nurse said as she left the room.

As soon as she was gone, Anastasia, Neil and Priscilla all appeared at the same time. China was a bit startled.

"All right, you guys," said Roni. "You can't just go around appearing and disappearing whenever you want. Just because we've already seen you doesn't mean it doesn't freak us out when you do that."

The guardians apologized briefly. They were too busy fussing over the baby.

"Angels," said Roni looking at China. "Can't teach them to act like humans, and you can't kill them."

China was frowning at her like she had cabbage growing out of her ears.

"That was a joke because you can't kill... Oh, never mind. So what are we going to name this baby?"

Roni picked the child up and handed her to China. The blond-haired girl sat for a few moments, staring down into the sweet little face. It was amazing that something so beautiful could come from a situation so vile. Trinity had left this precious life in her hands, and she would do her best to make her friend proud.

"Neil, what was my mother's name?"

Everyone in the room was silent. No one had expected her to ask that. The angel walked over to the bed and knelt down.

"Your mother—and Ryan's—was named Allyson. It means noble and beautiful."

"Then that's her name. Allyson Trinity Miller. You are beautiful, Allyson, and I love you." She kissed the baby on the forehead. Allyson squirmed a little and for a moment it looked like she smiled.

"Mom would say that's just gas," quipped Ryan, who had just come into the room.

Roni turned around and smacked him in the head.

"Hey Rapunzel, take it easy!"

"I just did what your mother would have done if she were here."

"Alright, alright," said Ryan. "I'm sorry for ruining the moment, but I need everyone to leave so I can talk to mom and baby in private."

Reluctantly, Roni and Priscilla left. Neil and Anastasia stayed but became invisible.

"Ok. We have to talk. You know Allyson is not technically your child."

China held the baby a little closer.

"I've talked to a detective and a social worker. They think they can get custody of the child turned over to my parents."

China's eyes grew wide, and the fear of losing her only link to Trinity made her heart begin to race. She started to feel faint but, before a full blown panic attack could consume her, Ryan touched her arm softly.

"Please don't worry," he assured her. "When you are stronger and more independent, my parents will release her back to you. She will be your daughter and, they hope, their granddaughter too."

China looked into her brother's eyes and wanted to believe him. She wanted to trust him. She suddenly felt her guardian's presence and decided to let go and remove one brick from her emotional wall. She wanted to let Ryan into the stronghold she had built around her heart. She nodded her head slowly.

"Do you know if you have a birth certificate? And, if you do, do you know what name is on it?"

She started to shake her head, but then a thought came to her.

"Maybe at the house. Joseph has a room with lots of books and papers," she said.

"Ok, well, that's going to have to wait then. How about a middle name for you? You got a name you always wanted?"

China was quiet. She had never really thought about her name. She had more pressing matters on her mind when she was growing up.

"Will you pick one for me?" she asked.

Ryan felt honored that she had asked him to do it, although he had always considered naming people a woman's job. He thought carefully so as not to say something stupid again.

"How about—Sharleen? It's my... our mother's name. I mean, our adoptive mother."

He felt like he was messing up again, but China looked pleased with the addition to her name. She said it out loud a couple of times and seemed happy with his choice. He took to writing some things down on his mound of papers and was busy for a few minutes. His concentration was broken when he heard China speaking again.

"Do we have a father?" she asked nervously.

Ryan looked up at her, trying to figure out how to answer her without somehow terrifying her.

"Well, yes. Remember? I mentioned him in the ambulance. His name is Greg and he is the best dad in the world. He never raised his voice at me my whole life. Even the night..."

His voice started to crack as he remembered the night Jason had died. His dad didn't yell at him or blame him for what had happened. In fact he went overboard to show his love to his son. He arranged for Ryan to fly out of

Wichita the next day, when he should have been at home comforting his mother and helping out at his brother's funeral.

"He never yells at people."

The words didn't come out right. Tears were welling up in his eyes, but he took a deep breath and held back his emotions. Then his sister did something that she hadn't done since he found her—she reached out and touched his hand. He felt her healing power flow through his body. His wounds—where Roni had shocked him—were gone and he could feel his ribs growing back together. But the biggest healing he could feel was in his heart.

The peace this girl gave him was indescribable. He finally understood what Jason and Roni had had.

CHAPTER 28

Shopping Spree

*"Submit yourselves therefore to God. Resist
the devil, and he will flee from you."*

James 4:7

Allyson's assessment at the hospital was coming to an
end. The social worker and pediatrician were satisfied
that she was a strong, healthy baby girl. She was almost
ready to go home but Ryan decided it would be best to
keep her—and China—for a few more days. At least until
his parents were able to meet with Madeline. A meeting
was being set up as soon as Michael thought it was safe for
them to come out of hiding. China only minimally
protested. She figured a few more days of rest would only
make her a better mother.

Ryan arranged it so that Allyson could stay in the
hospital with China. Juli would be staying in the hospital,
too, so she was moved into the same room as China and
the baby. The girls hit it off right away.

James and John were released into Michael's custody.
He took them out to the lake house so they could be well
looked after. Zoei went with them as well. She was happy
with that. On the drive out, all she could talk about with
the boys was Mr. U-ie and how he would give them piggyback rides.

Priel leaned over and said to Michael, "Someone is in
for some fun." They both laughed.

Ryan called Seth to ask if he and Solomon could go
and snoop around at Joseph's house to see what kind of

paperwork they could find on China. He also wanted to know how the repairs to the lake house were coming along. Seth reported that everything was under control and he expected to have the repairs done by Tuesday or Wednesday. He agreed to go over to Joseph's house and see what he and Solomon could find.

Roni decided that this was her cue to go shopping. She didn't get to go to Wichita too often, so this was an opportunity not to be missed. Jillian, not surprisingly, was excited about the shopping trip too.

Jeni and Jared, however, preferred to walk downtown on their own. They would look in the shops for a little while and maybe get something to eat. They didn't want to be away from Juli for too long. Roni gave Jeni the spare bank card.

"One hundred dollars. No more," she said to her sister. Jeni was satisfied with that and wanted to leave right away, before her big sister could change her mind.

"I'll try and get us some more bathroom stuff, so we don't have to use motel toothbrushes and shampoo again. Get yourself an outfit or two. And bring me receipts!" Roni yelled after her sister, but she had already left the room.

Roni and Jillian said their goodbyes to Juli and China and left for the mall. It was a sunshiny day, that Tuesday afternoon. The temperature was in the 40s, so they still needed to bundle up a bit. Priscilla and Raven had decided not to be seen or heard, but they would be close by if the girls needed them.

Their first stop at the mall—Maurice's—was Roni's favorite place to buy clothes. Jillian liked the shop too, so the two girls had a happy time trying on outfit after outfit.

Roni tried on ten pairs of jeans before she found two that she liked. She had lost a few pounds and was happy to be in a smaller size. She lost count of how many shirts she had put on; but the store was having a sale, so she didn't feel guilty for buying five of them. A three-pair pack of earrings would complete her outfits—or so she thought until she saw Jillian's pile.

"The clothes here are so great and they have all the accessories to go with them!" squealed Jillian. "Look at this hat. It's so adorable. And these scarves. Which one looks best on me? The blue? The red? Or the orange? Not the orange. Oh, this would look fabulous on one of your sisters. The one with the Russet Rose hair. I'm buying it for her!"

"The... what hair?"

"Russet Rose. It's a hair-dye color. Russet Rose number 48," said Jillian.

"Well, I can pretty much guarantee that her hair is a natural Rugged Rose number 48. She doesn't dye it."

"It's Russet Rose, silly. Wow, I can't believe that it's her natural color. It's brilliant! And here is a brown scarf for the one with Autumn Joy number 30 hair. Oh Roni, I've found the perfect hat for you. You have to try it on!"

Jillian went on and on like this for the whole hour and a half they were in the store. Roni ended up with more than her little three-pair pack of earrings for accessories. She almost choked when the cashier announced her bill.

"Two hundred and twenty-six dollars and fifty-seven cents."

"Jillian, if you ever tell my sisters what I spent here today, I swear I will pull out my flaming sword and use it on you."

Jillian laughed. "Your secret is safe with me. Besides, I wouldn't want to see you cry when I whip you in a duel."

The girls stopped at Wal-Mart to get some other girl's necessities. They eventually found themselves in the baby's section, looking at all the cute stuff they could get for Allyson. They were like two aunts setting out to spoil a favorite niece.

"Let's do a baby shower for China and Allyson!" Jillian suggested.

Roni thought it was an excellent idea. The two girls got shopping carts and filled them to the brim with clothes, toys, diapers, wipes, and all the other baby needs they could think of. Roni ordered a crib and matching dresser, to be delivered to the lake house on Wednesday.

"I hope she likes pink," said Jillian as she picked up a pink diaper bag with orange and brown trim.

"I have a feeling she will," Roni assured her. Just then she had a thought. "Maybe we should take China out for a makeover and some shopping tomorrow, if Ryan will release her for a couple of hours."

"That would be awesome!" squealed Jillian.

It was getting close to dinner time and Roni was beginning to tire from shopping. She was hoping that Jillian had satisfied some of her shopaholic needs for the day. They stopped by a little outdoor Mexican café to order some quesadillas and lemonade. The sun was beginning to go down and it was too cold to sit outside for long, so they took the food back with them to the car to eat. When they had finished their dinner, they drove back to the hospital. Jillian chattered away and Roni wondered if the girl would ever quit talking.

"You know, you have fabulous skin. You should let me do a makeover on you. It would be fun. Or maybe we could all go to the spa tomorrow and get facials and manicures and pedicures. We could get our hair done and..."

"Whoa, whoa, whoa!" said Roni. "I don't seem to recall a money tree at the lake house. I'm sure all that stuff would be fun but..."

"Oh no, silly, you wouldn't have to pay for it. My parents own a spa right out on the west edge of Wichita. My dad runs it because my mom has her own cosmetic surgery practice. In fact, I think one of her partners is going to be looking at China's mouth today. My parents are loaded, so they don't mind if we splurge on our friends. It's kind of nice that you didn't know about my parents before we became friends. The kids at my school know about our wealth and just want to be friends with me and Jared because our family has money."

Jillian was such a sweet girl. She never put on airs and acted like she was better than anyone else. Roni thought about most of the girls in her hometown. Snotty little rich kids who thought they were entitled to everything without having to work for it. They drove around in their new cars, sticking their noses up at anyone they thought was beneath them.

"So what do you think?"

Roni had been so deep in thought that she had missed the rest of what Jillian had said.

"Sorry, say that last part again."

"I said, what do you think about getting China to go to the spa with us tomorrow?"

"Yeah, that would be great, but we've got to get Dr Frankenstein to let his patient out of her cell first."

They both laughed.

"Leave that to me," said Jillian. "My dad says I could sell mining rights in a swamp!"

The girls continued to laugh as they pulled into the hospital parking lot. As they got out of the car, Roni looked up at the hospital building in the direction of China and Juli's room, which was the last one on the north side of the building. It was there that the hospital extension was being built. Out of the corner of her eye, she thought she saw a spark coming from the third floor of the extension. She looked again and saw another and then another. It was too late for the construction crews to be out working. Then the spot on her cheek started to glow and she cupped her hand over it and cried out.

"What is it, Roni?" asked Jillian as she went over and tried to relieve some of her friend's pain. But it was in vain. The burning could not be quenched.

"Tell me, what is the matter, Roni?"

Roni managed to catch her breath for just a moment, and she whispered one word.

"Ezekiel."

CHAPTER 29

Ezekiel Strikes Again

"Guard my life and rescue me; let me not be put to shame, for I take refuge in you."

Psalm 25:20, NIV

China and Juli had spent most of the afternoon playing checkers and Uno. Anastasia, Ariel and Neil took turns holding Allyson.

"This baby's feet are never going to touch the ground with the three of us around," said Anastasia.

"Perhaps we could teach her to fly," Ariel said jokingly.

"It's so hard to let them fall down when they are learning to walk," Anastasia said.

Neil added, "It's even worse when they are older and they fall. If it was only the ground they were falling to, life would be so much easier for them."

Dr Parker showed up at about 4pm to meet China and look at her lip. She was very kind and the girl liked her right away. She said the cleft lip could be easily fixed but she wanted to wait until China was stronger before she performed the surgery.

The doctor stayed a little while and played a round of checkers against Juli. China sat and watched her new-found friends as they played the game. She never knew there were so many nice people in the world. How was she so fortunate to have met so many in such a short time? Maybe the Creator that Neil and Anastasia were always talking about had made it happen.

"Hey China," said Juli, "You want to watch a movie?"

China's eyes grew wide with delight and she nodded her head eagerly. The hospital had a movie library where the patients could borrow movies to watch in their rooms. Juli called down to the nurse's station and asked if she could get one for her and China. They brought up *Tangled* and *Cars*.

"Well, that's a no-brainer," laughed Juli. She picked up *Tangled* and put it in the DVD player in the back of the TV. China held Allyson and fed her a bottle while they watched the movie.

The girls sat glued to the TV. China was amazed that Juli knew the words to every song in the movie. And she sang so well too. They had to play the song "At Last I See the Light" three times because it was Juli's favorite. As the movie ended, a nurse wearing a mask entered the room. He said he needed to take the baby to the nursery for a while to check her vitals.

"The doctor has already signed off on all her medical needs," said Juli. "You don't need to take her anywhere."

"I'm sorry," said the nurse, "but Dr Meiller said I needed to take the baby to the nursery."

The mispronunciation of such a common last name made Juli suspicious. China knew at once that the masked man was trying to cover up a Russian accent. She looked closely at his eyes. They were familiar. They were not the eyes of the man in the pictures in the hospital hallway. Those eyes made a person feel peaceful, while the eyes in the masked face before her made one feel afraid.

"The baby isn't going anywhere with you," said Juli.

"I'm sorry, miss, I'm just following orders," said the nurse nervously as he reached over and tried to take Allyson away from China.

Neil, Ariel and Anastasia began to walk over to the bed. It was clear this man had some kind of ulterior motive.

When he leaned over to grab Allyson, China reached her hand up and tore the mask off the nurse's face.

"You!" she cried. "What are you doing here?"

"I'm just following orders, China. Don't make this any harder than it has to be."

At that moment, China's cheek began to burn. She loosened her grip on Allyson for just a second as the pain engulfed her face. The man took the opportunity to grab his prize and run out of the room. As he left the room, Ezekiel came through the door. China screamed and fell out of her bed onto the floor.

Juli jumped out of her bed, ripping her IV out. She grabbed China and pulled her into the back corner of the room. She began to sing softly into the ear of the terrified girl to calm her.

Ezekiel and the three angels began to fight in the small room. Suddenly Anastasia disappeared. She reappeared in the hallway. She was searching for her charge, but something was blocking her connection with the child. She was just about to go through the doors that led to the construction area when Ryan and Oriel came running around the corner.

"Ezekiel is here," she said, "and someone has taken the baby."

Ryan hit his chest and shouted, "The sword of the Lord!"

Swords in their hands, he and Oriel burst through the swinging doors and out onto the construction site. The enemy was waiting at the far end. A slew of small, flaming darts were making their way toward Ryan's head. He ducked behind a large pile of plywood and dodged them just in time.

"Use your shield, Ryan!" shouted Oriel from his hiding place opposite Ryan.

"What shield?" Ryan yelled back as he narrowly escaped another dart that was meant for his head.

"The one on your left arm."

"What?" said Ryan. "I don't see anything!"

"You can't see it. You have to have faith that it is there and it will be," the angel instructed him.

"Oh, that makes sense. Guess that's why it's called the Shield of Faith. That's some important information that would have been nice to know... let's say, two minutes ago," Ryan muttered to himself.

Ryan took a deep breath and looked at Oriel, who was now positioned behind a large support pillar. They both nodded and took off running towards the onslaught of flaming darts.

"In the name of the Lord!" they both shouted.

To Ryan's amazement, the arrows hit his invisible shield and bounced off it. They made shimmering ripples on the surface of the shield, like when you throw a rock into a pond. The darts fell to the ground and disappeared before his eyes.

This time their attackers were not the enormous Nephilim but short, red-faced, devilish-looking creatures with scraggly bat wings. Each demon had a small crossbow that never seemed to run out of ammunition.

"Aim for their heads!" shouted Oriel. "Once their heads are cut off, their spirits will return to the Dark One's domain."

"That sounds easy enough," Ryan said to himself. "Chop off their heads, they go bye-bye."

They finally reached the demons closest to them. The little goblin-like creatures were no match for Ryan and Oriel's swords. They screeched at the sight of the two warriors and spat their poisonous venom at them. A drop hit the toe of Ryan's boot and smoke came up where it landed. He could feel the heat going all the way into his foot.

"That's going to hurt for a while," he said as he tried to kick the venom off his boot. The poison stuck fast. He could not get rid of it. He would just have to fight on, despite this minor annoyance. He was beginning to think those menacing demons were just an annoying distraction to keep him and Oriel busy.

"I think so too," said Oriel.

"What? Oh yeah, the mind-reading thing again. Let's finish these guys off and go find the real danger."

Ryan and Oriel cut down the small army of demons in just ten minutes.

"Now what?" said Ryan.

"Let's go forward and see what these creatures were keeping us from," answered Oriel.

They walked slowly through the unfinished building, their swords in their hands. A cold November breeze was causing the plastic sheeting to billow up in the air. Every noise they heard made them stop and listen. After a while, Oriel stood up straight. He was just about to say "there is no one here" when, out of the corner of his eye, he saw a blue light coming toward Ryan. The guardian lunged forward and knocked his charge to the ground. The blue ball of light hit the wall near the doors. It left a black burn mark where it landed.

"What in the world? Roni?" Ryan was trying to figure out what had just happened.

"It's not Roni," the protector said. "It's someone else."

Out of the shadows appeared a girl. She was built short and muscular, like Roni. She had short brown spiky hair and her eyes were glowing blue. Ryan couldn't believe his eyes. He could see that her hands were smoldering from the blue fireball she had just thrown. He thought he saw a tear in her eye.

"Who are you?" asked Ryan, who was still feeling stunned.

"I am Sarah," the AIRborn said.

Oriel stood up and faced the frightened girl. He spoke softly to her. "What do you want, my child?"

"To be well," she replied. "My master says I need this man and the girl Roni to be well again."

"Who is your master?" asked Ryan; but he already knew the answer to his question.

"Ezekiel is my master," she stated and began to glow blue again.

Ryan quickly put his shield up, just in time. She threw several more volleys of blue fire at him, but the shield was able to deflect them.

When it seemed like she was spent, Ryan lowered his shield, thinking it would be safe to try to talk to her. But he was mistaken. As soon as his head came in view, she began to shoot fireballs at him again.

"What is up with this girl?" said Ryan to Oriel.

"It would seem as though Ezekiel has deceived her," Oriel answered.

Ryan looked over at Oriel and all he could say was, "You think?!"

CHAPTER 30

A Beam of Light

*"The entrance of thy words giveth light; it
giveth understanding unto the simple."*

Psalm 119:130

Anastasia decided to go the opposite way to search for
Allyson. She looked in every room down the third floor
hallway. She kept her ears open for the cry of a baby. As
she was about to head down the stairs, Jeni and Jared
came out of the elevator. One look at Anastasia's face told
them that something was wrong. No words were
exchanged as Jeni, Jared and their guardians ran towards
the girls' room.

Jeni was almost to Juli's room. She decided it was
time for her to join in the spiritual warfare. She stopped
and hit her chest. "The sword of the Lord!" she said aloud.

Immediately, she was in full battle gear. In her hand
was a golden bow. A quiver hung down her back, and it
was full of arrows with silver tips and white feathers. A
dagger hung from her waistband.

"Sweet! Just like Katniss."

Jared and the two guardians caught up with her. His
swords were drawn. He smiled when he saw Jeni's
spiritual armor.

"God is angry with the wicked every day," he said. "He
will whet his sword; he hath bent his bow, and made it
ready. (*Psalm 7:11-12*)"

"Are we all ready?" asked Jeni. Everyone nodded in
agreement. "Then let's do this!"

"In the name of the Lord!" exclaimed Samuel and Camiel, as loud as a whisper could be.

"That's what she meant," said Jared.

They crept up to the door of the girls' room. Ezekiel, Neil and Ariel were going at it pretty hard. Jeni could see Juli and China huddled in the far corner of the room.

"I got this." She stood up and positioned herself in the doorway. She pulled out two arrows and drew back her string. "Hey angel cakes, I got a message from the Lord for you."

She released the string. The tips of the two arrows burst into flames and hit Ezekiel on either side of his spine, near the shoulder blades. He whipped around and saw the warrior girl standing in the doorway.

"It's the other redhead. Come closer, my dear, and my sword will give you a message from my master, the Shining One."

Jeni had distracted him enough, so Neil could sneak up on him and plunge his sword into Ezekiel's back and straight through his heart.

Ezekiel shrieked and then disappeared. Everyone was shocked.

"That was too easy," said Samuel.

"Easy?" Neil replied.

Jeni ran over to her sister, who was still singing as she huddled in the corner with China.

"Juli, I'm here. You are safe. I'm here."

Juli looked up at her twin and said, "I was in no danger. We were well protected."

China was mumbling something that Jeni couldn't make out. The guardians lifted the two girls back into bed.

Juli's arm was bleeding where her IV had been pulled out. Neil sat on the edge of China's bed and stroked her hair gently and sang softly to her.

***

Anastasia was still trying to find the man who had taken the baby. She searched every floor frantically, till at last she found herself at ground level. She saw Jillian and Roni drive by. She tried to yell for them but she was too late. She ran toward the parking lot after them. She didn't use her angel powers to catch up with them because she didn't want to miss the baby if she was somewhere nearby.

She could see Jillian and Roni getting out of the car. They were looking up at the blue light coming from the third floor of the hospital extension. Then she saw Roni holding her cheek.

"Jillian! Roni!" she shouted.

Jillian turned and saw her running toward them. Anastasia quickly told them and their guardians what had happened. Jillian had taken hold of Roni's face. She kept trying to take the pain away from her.

"Roni, you must cry out to the Creator! He is the only one who can help you!" advised Anastasia.

Roni knew that Anastasia was right. "Creator, help me!" she cried out. Immediately the pain left her.

The angels and the two girls geared themselves up for battle as they made their way to the ground floor of the hospital extension. Anastasia, Raven and Jillian entered the construction site on the left, while Roni and Priscilla went to the right.

All was quiet on the left of the construction area. Then, out of a door of the half-completed building, a nurse came running. He was carrying a grocery bag and heading for an old, brown hatchback car. Jillian, Raven and Anastasia leapt over to where the man was trying frantically to fit a key into the car door.

"Going somewhere?" Raven asked.

The man nearly fainted away.

"Give us the child and we will spare your life."

"We will?" Jillian and Anastasia said at the same time and looked at Raven.

"Fine," said Anastasia. "We will."

The frightened man handed the grocery bag over to Anastasia. She looked inside but Allyson wasn't there. Raven put his sword to the man's throat.

"What is your business here, little man?"

The man swallowed hard. He was too frightened to speak.

"I think we should tie him up and question him later," said Jillian. "It's obvious he's too scared to talk now." She motioned down to the ground near the man's feet, where a puddle had formed.

"Obviously," said Raven.

Anastasia grabbed the man by his scrubs and lifted him two feet off the ground.

"Where is the baby, you worthless human!"

He tried speaking once again but all he could do was point to the hospital building. Jillian and Raven convinced Anastasia to put the man down before she killed him. She took off toward the building.

They tied his wrists behind his back with a piece of thin wire they had found at the construction site. Raven wrapped it around several times in a figure eight to make sure their prisoner couldn't get away.

"You should be thankful that you're alive," Raven said to the man. "Guardians have killed for a lot less." He looked over to Jillian. "Where are we going to keep him until we can question him properly?"

She looked around and saw the very thing they were looking for. She grinned as she pointed to a portable toilet. The irony was very appropriate and they both had a good laugh as they walked the man over to the small prison. Jillian taped his mouth shut with duct tape.

"You might not want to rock this outhouse too much in an effort to escape," Jillian said. "I don't think it's been serviced for a few days. It would be... unfortunate if you tipped it over."

Jillian and Raven shut the door and were able to lock it from the outside. They spotted a can of orange spray paint nearby that was being used to mark pipelines. Jillian picked it up and wrote OUT OF ORDER on the door of the portable toilet.

"Now let us go join our brothers in their fight," said Raven.

"Don't forget about our sisters too," Jillian reminded him.

"Of course, our sisters too."

***

Roni and Priscilla entered the construction site cautiously. They could hear a huge racket going on a few floors up. There were piles of sheetrock and plywood everywhere. The walls of plastic sheeting made it difficult to see very far, and Roni had to be careful that her flaming sword didn't come into contact with any of it and set the plastic on fire.

They crept slowly along through the maze of building materials. Priscilla took her sword and moved a sheet of plastic out of their way so they could see into the next area. There was no one there.

They went through two more rooms. Then Priscilla pointed to a soft glow coming from the east side of the building. Slowly they made their way toward the light, keeping a careful watch all the time.

When Roni pulled back the last barrier between them and the source of the light, her eyes were immediately drawn to several powerful work lamps positioned across from each other. There were four on each side of the makeshift room, all pointing to a single space. The glare blinded Roni and Priscilla as they stepped into the room. A low laugh came from the far corner.

"I see you have returned to me again, my daughter," said Ezekiel with a smirk on his face.

"Nice to see you again, Pops," Roni glared at the fallen angel. "What do you want from me this time? I thought I made it clear that I wasn't going anywhere with you."

"I want to make a trade. I have something you want, and you have something I want," said Ezekiel.

Once again he was trying to barter for her life.

"I'm sure you have nothing I want," Roni shouted back.

"Oh, I believe I do."

He held up a small pink blanket like a sling. In the fold of the blanket, suspended in the air, was Allyson. She was not crying. She was just looking around with her wide blue eyes.

Roni wanted to rush at the evil angel but Priscilla held her back. She touched her sword to Roni's shoulder, causing the young human to take a deep breath and consider what was before her. She needed to proceed with great caution.

"Do you hear that sound upstairs?" bellowed Ezekiel. It is another AIRborn like you. She has pinned down your human, the good doctor. He will not survive much longer."

Upon hearing this, Roni made a quick decision to deal with her opponent. He had the high ground now.

"What do you want?" she asked and took a step forward, focusing her gaze on Ezekiel. She tried to keep his attention on her as Priscilla began to sidestep around to the back of the lights.

"You know what I want. I want you and your doctor. I have other children who need his expertise."

She took another step forward.

"I see. If you need him, you should call off the assault on him and his guardian."

She knew Oriel would be fighting right alongside Ryan. She was trembling from head to toe, but she didn't want Ezekiel to see her terror. Unconsciously she began to feel for her necklace. Ryan had given it back after the last meeting with this evil predator. She could see her guardian closing in on him.

A gust of air circled through the plastic room and Roni caught a glimpse of Anastasia as the sheeting rose with the swell of the wind. The guardian was positioning herself opposite Priscilla.

Roni stepped forward again. She was almost to the center of the lights. She could barely see Ezekiel now, but she knew he was smiling, thinking he had won. She took her eyes off him for a moment and looked down at the charm she was holding between her fingers. She closed her eyes to say a prayer to the Creator.

"Save me, O God, by thy name," she whispered. "Hear my prayer, O God; give ear to the words of my mouth. For strangers are risen up against me, and oppressors seek after my soul: they have not set God before them... Behold, God is mine helper: the Lord is with them that uphold my soul. (*Psalm 54:1-4*)"

Roni was strengthened by the words of the psalmist. She opened her eyes to look at the crystal in her hand and saw what looked like a black spot on her palm. For a moment, she thought that she had ink on her hand. The charm rolled a little as she tried to rub the spot away with her thumb, but the stain was gone.

Again she studied the pendant and saw that the same black marks had reappeared on her palm. She began to realize that the light from the lamps was causing the crystal to show what looked like impurities in its structure. She thought she saw some letters forming on her palm. G. Then, next to that, an E. Next was an N, then another E.

"It must have a word etched in it," she thought.

She tried sounding out what she had so far. A name perhaps. Gene?

"Who is Gene?" she wondered.

The letters weren't making a complete word, so she went to the next letter. S, then I, then another S.

"Genesis," she said aloud.

Ezekiel had been taunting her this whole while. He was trying to scare her into surrendering. But, when he heard her utter the word Genesis, he was the one who started to tremble. He tried to get her attention but he could not.

Suddenly a verse came into Roni's mind.

"The entrance of thy words giveth light. (*Psalm 119:130*)." She kept saying the verse over and over again, trying to figure out what it meant. "The entrance of thy words giveth light."

Ezekiel was beginning to get frantic and Roni could see his desperation. She remembered how he had grabbed the necklace off Ryan when it had begun to glow, out at the lake house. It had burned a hole right through his hand. A thought came to her and she took the necklace off. She stepped forward and held it toward the center of the beams of light.

All at once she was surrounded by words. They were being projected onto the plastic walls surrounding the room. She looked for the G that began the word Genesis. She found it and began to read.

"In the beginning God created the heaven and the earth. And the earth was without form, and void; and darkness was upon the face of the deep. And the Spirit of

God moved upon the face of the waters. And God said, Let there be light. (*Genesis 1:1-3*)"

Something was happening to the necklace as Roni read those words. A powerful beam, ten times brighter than what was already there, shot out toward Ezekiel. He was already trying to escape the words that were coming from the necklace. If any touched him, it would pierce a hole through his whole body.

He shrieked loudly and released the pink blanket with Allyson in it. Both Priscilla and Anastasia dove for the precious bundle. Priscilla caught the baby before she hit the ground. She immediately handed Allyson over to her grateful guardian, who was weeping tears of joy for her safe return.

The beam of light grew more and more intense until it consumed Ezekiel's entire body. As he disintegrated into what looked like dust, he looked at Roni and shouted, "This is not over. I still have something that you want."

"You have nothing I want or need."

"We will see," he laughed. "We will see."

Then what sounded like a sonic boom shook the building, and he was gone from their sight once more.

CHAPTER 31

Sarah

"But whoso hath this world's good, and seeth his brother have need, and shutteth up his bowels of compassion from him, how dwelleth the love of God in him?"

1 John 3:17

Ryan and Oriel were still pinned down on the third floor. Sarah's volley of blue flames was relentless. She, like Roni, gained strength the longer she fought. Ryan tried to reason with her.

"Please, Sarah, I can help you. I know how to fix your pacemaker so you will be able to live a long life. I also know how to make the medication you will need to stop the nanites in your body from attacking it."

Sarah paused for a moment to consider what this man was saying to her. She wanted to give up and believe he could save her, but Ezekiel had her brother. She had to save him, and the only way to do that was to get this doctor and the girl.

"I'm sorry but I can't give up. You must surrender to me so I can present you to Ezekiel."

She began to fire at them again.

"Doesn't this girl have a guardian who could help us out?" said Ryan to Oriel.

At that moment, a small angel appeared and crouched down next to Ryan. He nearly jumped out of his skin.

"Ahh! You guys have to stop doing that," he said. "You're going to give me a heart attack!"

"I'm very sorry but you asked where I was, so I thought I'd make my presence known. I'm Rachel, Sarah's guardian."

Once Ryan had caught his breath, he asked Rachel why Sarah was so bent on capturing him when he had said he could help her.

"Ezekiel has her brother, Adam. He is a prisoner in the Norilsk facility in Russia. Ezekiel has promised to heal her heart as well as her brother's if she will help him capture you and Roni."

"Can she be reasoned with?"

"She has been tortured for months now and her powers are unstable. It is really too early for her to start using them. Her physical body isn't ready."

"So her heart hasn't stopped like Roni's did?" asked Ryan.

"No, not yet. She is only thirteen. Ezekiel designed an electric bed for Sarah and these other so-called children of his. He straps them to it and gradually increases the amount of electricity flowing into their bodies, until they begin to exhibit their powers, thereby prematurely activating the nanites. They are attacking her heart even as we speak."

Ryan thought for a moment, then turned around and stood up in front of Sarah. She was about to shoot her fireballs at him again.

"Wait, Sarah, I know about your brother and I can help him too."

The girl paused for a moment, then shot back, "He said you would say that. You're lying! You don't care about anybody but yourself. Ezekiel told me all about you and your brother. You let him die when you had the power to save him. No wonder he didn't want to be your guardian anymore."

"What?" Ryan was stunned.

Did she just say Ezekiel used to be his guardian? How could that be? He looked at Oriel. Then he connected the dots. Ezekiel must have been his guardian before Jason died. Then Oriel could have transferred from Jason to him. That must have been how Ezekiel knew about Roni in the first place. He was near her for the first twelve years of her life.

"You have a lot of explaining to do later," he said to Oriel. Then he looked back at Sarah. "Please, I was just a child then. I didn't understand the repercussions of my actions. Since my brother died, I have dedicated my life to figuring out what happened.

"I found a drawing of a machine that can help you and hopefully your brother too. Ezekiel is using you to get to Roni. He doesn't care about you or your brother or anyone else at that facility. Once he has her, he will destroy you and anyone else that stands in his way."

Sarah's eyes were turning brown again. Ryan's voice was so kind and soft that she found herself daring to believe what he was saying.

"Is this all true?" she said to her guardian, who was standing near her now. "Can he do it? Will he keep his word and help Adam?"

Rachel stroked Sarah's face tenderly and said, "Of course he will, child."

Sarah began to let down her guard. She started crying. Then everyone felt a loud sonic boom and heard Ezekiel's voice coming from out of thin air: "This is not over. I still have something that you want!"

Sarah was terrified again. Her eyes began to glow blue and she was levitating about twelve inches off the ground. She threw a ball of light at her guardian, who disappeared before her eyes. Ryan and Oriel took cover.

Jeni and Samuel came rushing through the doors. Sarah fired at them both, but Samuel wrapped himself around Jeni and put up his shield. The balls of light dispersed on contact with the shield. Jeni managed to get off a few shots at Sarah, but they were blown away well before they could reach their intended target. The Russian girl kept firing at will for at least five minutes. The entire third floor was nearly destroyed.

***

After Ezekiel had disappeared, Roni began to make her way to the third floor. She could hear this other AIRborn still trying to get Ryan. As long as she could hear her blasting away, she knew he was still safe.

There was scaffolding next to the south end of the construction site. She decided to make her ascent there. Although she was in her battle gear, she found it remarkably easy to maneuver up the ladders.

Roni got to the third floor. She had come up right behind Sarah. She could see Jeni at the other end of the room, trying to shoot Sarah down.

"Nice bow and arrow," she thought.

Roni pulled herself up onto the floor. Then she stood quietly next to a beam, waiting for Jeni to get a hit—or at least distract the girl long enough for Roni to reach her kill switch. It only took a minute or two for that moment to come. Jeni had taken to firing two to three flaming arrows at once. Finally, one grazed Sarah's shoulder. That was Roni's cue to charge. She was only about fifteen feet from Sarah, and she covered the distance quite easily. The thought of what she was about to do made her cringe, but she knew it had to be done. She ran and hit Sarah in the back. Sarah screamed, her body convulsed in agony. Roni knew how much pain the girl was in, so she caught her and laid her on the floor gently. She began to cry as the young girl lost consciousness.

CHAPTER 32

A Long Road Ahead

*"LORD, you have assigned me my portion and my
cup; you have made my lot secure. The boundary
lines have fallen for me in pleasant places; surely I
have a delightful inheritance. I will praise the Lord,
who counsels me; even at night my heart instructs
me. I have set the LORD always before me. Because
he is my right hand, I will not be shaken."*

Psalm 16:5-8, NIV

Ryan ran over to Roni. He knelt on the ground, put his
arms around her, and held her tight.

"Is the baby safe?" Ryan asked.

"Yes, she is with her mother now," Priscilla assured
him.

He breathed a sigh of relief and inquired if anyone
else was injured. Nothing but a few cuts and bruises,
although his own foot was aching terribly from the
demon's venom that had dripped onto it.

"Let Michael look at that as soon as he returns," said
Priscilla. "Red demon venom is nothing to play around
with. It takes a little supernatural medication to heal a
wound like that."

Roni was still holding Sarah in her arms. She
wondered if there was anything that could help her. Ryan
examined the young girl carefully. Roni assisted him.
When she saw the bruise she had given Sarah on her back,
she started to weep. Ryan tried to comfort her but Roni
could not be consoled.

"I don't have another pacemaker ready yet," he said at last. "She is so young and her nanites were activated too early. I don't think it would help her anyway. I'm afraid the damage is irreversible. I'm going to have my staff run the same tests I had them perform on you. Maybe she still has a chance."

Rachel came over and lifted Sarah up. Ryan cleared a path and they brought her into the hospital. Roni decided to stay with Sarah during the tests.

Ryan went over to see China and Juli. He examined them carefully. Juli was going to need stitches where her IV was torn out but, other than that, she was fine. China was emotionally upset but had no physical injuries. She was being treated for shock. Ryan could hear her mumbling, "I know where I saw him..."

***

Ryan left the girls' room and ran into Michael as he came around the corner of the hallway.

"I hear I missed a big fight," said the Archangel.

"Yeah, you did," Ryan said. "Are we ever going to be rid of that Ezekiel character? Will he ever die?"

"Angels do not have eternal souls like humans. Like I said, we can only temporarily weaken them and put them in a holding cell; but, unless they choose to give up their *essentia*, they will never be fully conquered until the Creator Himself destroys them. That is why we must always be ready to do battle against the Dark One and his forces."

Ryan understood.

"I have just had a short meeting with Jillian and Raven downstairs in the parking lot. It seems they apprehended the nurse who stole Allyson. They had tied him up and kept him safe for questioning but, when they came back for him, he was dead."

"Well, that's just great," said Ryan. "Now we'll never know who he was."

"We already do know who he was. It was Janes."

Ryan was stunned. "Janes? How can that be? He helped us when we were in Norilsk."

"He must have been working for Ezekiel the whole time. It's obvious that he's the one who led Ezekiel and his forces to you and Roni."

"I figured out how to make the pacemaker and the medication. The information must be protected at all costs. If he gets hold of it, there's no telling how many children like Roni and Sarah he can control."

"I have already put Uriel on it. He guarded the Tree of Life in the Garden of Eden; he will not fail us. I may have to provide Roni—and Sarah, if she lives—extra guardians."

"That sounds like the appropriate thing to do. Ezekiel said he had more children. I assume he meant more young people like Roni."

"Yes," said Michael. "I wonder just how many children out there have these destructive powers. China said the facility began to shut down when she was eight. We can assume that the youngest of these children would be about ten years old."

"And the oldest would be no more than eighteen or nineteen," Ryan added.

"Looks like we have a long road ahead of us. Are you ready to go all the way in this fight for the human soul?"

Ryan looked Michael in the eye. The man and the Archangel locked arms. Ryan spoke with confidence.

"I will praise the LORD, who counsels me; even at night my heart instructs me. I have set the LORD always before me. Because he is at my right hand, I will not be shaken. (*Psalm 16:7-8, NIV*)"

"In the name of the Lord?" Michael asked Ryan.

"In the name of the Lord."

***

Neil was still singing to China when she finally started to come around. He smiled as he looked down on her.

"I am happy you are safe," he said to her.

"Me too," she smiled up at him. "Neil, I remember where I saw the man. The one in the painting. I saw him again today. He was keeping me and Juli safe from Ezekiel. When I was a child, he would come to me in my dreams and we would talk. He said he would always watch out for me even when bad things happen."

"I am glad for you, my child. The Creator's Son himself has fellowshipped with you."

"He says I will go and live with him someday, but he still has things for me to do here."

"Like taking care of Allyson?"

"Yes. How did you know?"

"Just a good guess. Now you need to rest so we can take you home soon."

He remembered something else he had to tell her.

"China, you don't have to worry about Janes anymore. He has his reward."

Roni stretched and yawned as she began to wake up. She forgot where she was for a moment, then she turned her head and saw Sarah lying in the bed next to her. The girl had so many IVs and wires connected to her that the nurses hadn't bothered to put a gown on her. She was covered only with a white sheet.

Roni got up and went over to her. She touched the sleeping girl's bandaged hand.

"I wish I had the power to heal you," she thought. "My powers only cause destruction."

Sarah began to stir. She opened her eyes slowly and looked at Roni. She tried to speak, but her mouth was dry. Roni found her some water and helped her to drink a little. When she had had sufficient, she laid her head back down on the bed.

Ryan entered the room just then and beheld the sweetest vision he had ever seen. The sun was just coming up and it was shining on Roni's hair. As she leaned over his patient, she looked like an angel of mercy. He watched her for a few moments. Finally she looked up and noticed him. There were tears in her eyes. He came over to her and put his hand on her back.

Sarah started to talk. "I know you," she said to Roni.

"Me? How can that be?" Roni inquired.

"I don't know," she said quietly.

It was silent in the room again for a few minutes while Ryan checked her chart.

"Can you really help my brother?" she asked Ryan.

"I will do my best. Where is he being held captive?"

"I don't know," she said. "But there are lots of other kids there. They have powers like me. Many of us have already died because of Ezekiel. He wants you two badly. He will not quit till he gets what he wants."

Her heart monitor started to beep a little faster.

"Please, you have to help my brother. He is not well." Her heart was racing now.

"Calm down, Sarah. You have to stay calm. The pacemaker isn't finished yet, and it's the only thing that can save you. Try and breathe slowly."

Ryan was doing his best to calm the girl down but his attempts were in vain.

"I can't save you yet!" he cried.

"Save my brother," she cried, grasping his hand.

She began to pant softly, as she felt her heart about to explode. She looked up at Roni one last time.

"I know... your face. A man... a prisoner... in the... facility. H...h... he... had a pic... picture of you. He said he was... your..."

"My what!" Roni leaned over Sarah's face and shouted. "My what?"

"He s... s... said he was your... father."

The heart monitor flat-lined.

"Where is he?! Where is my father?!" Roni screamed at the girl.

But she was already gone.

The End